Last First Kiss

Last First Kiss

A Legacy of the Maguires Romance

Stella Holt

TULE
PUBLISHING

Dedication

This book is dedicated to my mom and every widow missing a little romance.

Chapter One

CHARLOTTE TUCKED HER flowy blouse into the back of her pencil skirt for the tenth time that morning and vowed to never buy the fabric again. Glancing at the clock on her computer, she had a few minutes before her weekly call with the head of PR in New York. Then she could take a break from marketing metadata and go for a run along the river in her hometown of Alexandria, Virginia. Living outside of D.C. had its perks, with access to museums and amazing trails, but in the last year, Charlotte usually traveled for work too much to take advantage. It was fall, her favorite time of year. The air was crisp and the leaves were various shades of orange and yellow, so she didn't mind being home for a few days before her next assignment.

The buzzing sound of her alarm brought her back to the moment, and she smoothed her always frizzy hair back before answering the incoming virtual call.

"Hello, Renee. How's the weather up there?" Charlotte said, taking in her boss's beauty on the screen.

Renee's short dark hair was perfectly styled straight in a bob that hung against her chin. Her green eyes were framed by smoky eyeliner, and her lips were painted a deep red. In comparison, Charlotte's washed-out skin and dull hazel eyes seemed more apparent in the small box reflecting her image.

"I have a proposition for you," Renee said, pinning her eyes on Charlotte through the screen.

"I'm worried," she said as she fiddled with her rose-gold stapler.

"How would you like to join the team here in the New York office? I've convinced management to create a director of global PR and marketing position. You would work for me directly and have control over managing Cavalier's worldwide marketing plan."

"Me?"

"Last time we spoke you said you were interested in a change. It would mean less travel and no living out of a suitcase. The only question is how big of a change do you want?"

Excitement rolled down Charlotte's spine; this was exactly what she needed, not to mention a great opportunity. Then the guilt of wanting anything else waded in.

"Move to New York?" She voiced the idea out loud mostly to herself.

"After everything you've been through, I thought you might like the idea of a permanent change." Renee huffed, "You're the perfect person for the job."

"Is there an official vacancy I should apply to?" Charlotte asked, gulping at the rush of worry that followed her declaration.

"There will be soon. In the meantime, you could try to grease the skids with the new VP for the Field PR teams, Caleb Kincaid, do you know him?"

"What new VP?" Charlotte asked, sitting up straighter in

her chair.

"You must have missed the announcement; check your email. He was introduced today at the managers' meeting. He'll be overseeing all your fieldwork and probably won't be too happy about me poaching you." There was a long pause. "Charlotte, are you still there?"

Renee's voice jolted her out of her stalker-style scrolling on the company website.

There was a picture of a striking man next to an updated post about his recent promotion and move to New York. She couldn't help but study his square jaw, dark full eyebrows on a familiar handsome face, and permanent bronze skin tone. Charlotte's pulse was pounding, and her body betrayed her just as acutely as it had the first time she'd met Caleb Kincaid five years ago. He looked more like a model than a corporate vice president.

"I'm sorry, you were saying?" Charlotte said, looking away from the picture on her extra-large monitor in her home office. Instead, she focused on reorganizing her sticky notes.

"Look, don't worry about him. I just want to confirm you're interested before I start making the hard sell. I'll have to push HR to get this salary package put together and advertise the new position, then we can worry about Kincaid."

Charlotte exhaled the breath she'd been holding. "Great plan. Thank you for thinking of me."

"Are you kidding? This will be a game changer for my social life. Maybe with you by my side I can start working sixty hours a week instead of eighty. Enjoy your holiday weekend. Ciao for now." Renee hung up before Charlotte could respond.

A move from Virginia to New York offered a clean break, a fresh start. It was like a neon sign pointing north. She just had to get the job and convince her family it was for the best.

✕

THAT AFTERNOON ON the drive to her parents' lake house all Charlotte could think about was the potential job in New York. Even the holiday traffic was almost pleasurable as she considered how different her life would be in a new city. Highways faded into two-lane roads surrounded by tall rust-colored trees, but she was too distracted to enjoy them. The Maguire Family Lake Trip had been an annual Columbus Day Weekend event ever since Charlotte was a kid. Her parents would pack up her and her three rowdy brothers and drive to Lake Anna, to the log cabin her grandfather built.

The sound of the crunching stone driveway under her car tires brought back memories of years past like a scent could take a person back in time. The weathered cabin with light gray shingles and white shutters was surrounded by mature oak trees that stretched into the sky. There was always a cool breeze rolling off the lake, and if she stared long enough, she could see a fish jump out of the water. It was late afternoon, and the sun was slowly making its descent over the tops of the trees. For the last few years she'd managed to skip the trip, but this year she was facing the family tradition head-on.

After the tragic death of her husband Sam two years ago, she had dodged any family event she could. It was too painful to be flooded with memories while everyone treated her like a piece of delicate glass that might break any minute.

She'd been the first of her siblings to marry, but Sam had already been entrenched in her family as her oldest brother Rory's best friend and the boy next door growing up. His death impacted everyone in her family as if he were one of their own. But it was time everyone, including her, stopped seeing her as the sad police widow and accepted Sam was gone. She needed to step out of the cloud that hung over her; moving to New York sounded like the best way to do that. In her hometown, everyone knew she was a widow but in New York, she could just be Charlotte again.

Sitting in her parked car, she looked out over the white picket fence that separated the driveway from the lush green yard. She spotted her brothers sitting on the red and white striped lawn chairs already relaxed and enjoying the sun. Knowing they would trapse up the lawn if she didn't get out of the car soon, she took a deep breath, and opened her door. Her middle brother, Conner, popped out of his seat and waved unabashedly in ripped jeans and a sleeveless shirt. His hair was too long, and he looked like he belonged in a grunge band, which was exactly the point as an undercover D.C. police officer.

"Hey, get your suit on stat," Conner called out. "Finn and Rory have challenged us to a relay race on the lake, and the losers have to cook tonight."

"Why do you let them trick you every time?" Charlotte yelled back as she grabbed her bag from the trunk.

There was music playing on the outdoor speakers and her other two brothers sat with cocky smirks as Conner walked closer.

Once he was in earshot Conner leaned over the picket fence with a conspiratorial grin. "They each have to swim with one arm tied behind their backs," he said as if that would guarantee them a win.

"One Navy SEAL and a coast guard certified rescue swimmer. You're a sucker!" Charlotte said.

"Don't underestimate my skills," Conner hollered back over his shoulder as he walked toward the lake, but their brothers' booming laughter followed.

Heaving her weekend bag up the wood steps, she opened the front door painted a cheery red, and stepped inside the cool newly remodeled cabin. Light wood floors, crisp white walls, and nautical accents decorated the entryway. It was still the old family cabin but with a chic, modern update. Her mom had harassed her father for years to let her remodel the cabin and she'd finally won.

"Charlotte, is that you?" her mom called out from the kitchen.

"Hi, Mom," she called, dropping her bag at the door and walking down the hallway that opened into the kitchen and family room combo. Her mom was standing at a new farmhouse sink in her swanky remodeled kitchen outfitted with navy blue cabinets and white marble countertops. Charlotte had seen pictures, but this was her first time seeing the changes in person. "It's so pretty in here. Do you even go outside now?"

Her mom's smile pushed laugh lines into her cheeks, and

her hazel eyes sparkled. "I do love my new kitchen, but nothing beats sitting out on the deck." Wiping her hands on the towel tucked into her apron, her mom walked around the island to give Charlotte a big hug. "Especially when I have all four of my babies here. I'm so glad you could make it." Her mom kissed her cheek.

Charlotte grabbed a cookie off a cooling rack before her mom could shoo her out of the kitchen.

"Go get your suit on and enjoy the lake before the sun sets," her mom ordered. "The boys have the paddleboards out already, but you might want your rash guard because I'm betting that water is chilly."

"Yes, Mom." Charlotte ate the cookie in two bites.

Grabbing her bag from the front door, she moved to the first bedroom off the hallway that had two bunk beds. Her mom's not-so-subtle attempt in the remodel to remind her four adult children that she expected grandkids sooner than later. Previously she would have stayed in one of the larger rooms with Sam, but he was gone and it was time for new traditions.

"You ready to get your butt whooped in the lake?" her oldest brother Rory called through the door. He knocked before barging into her room.

"It's nice to see you too," Charlotte said as she unzipped and dug through her suitcase to find her bathing suit.

Rory grinned and hugged her. "Why'd you drive up alone?"

"I had to work today, and I need to leave early Monday for my next job in Vancouver."

He nodded but looked at her like he would find another

7

reason in her eyes.

"Have you given any more thought about getting a local PR position that doesn't require so much travel?" Rory asked.

As the oldest, he was always looking out for his three younger siblings and offering advice. Rory was a police officer too and he was the sergeant on the same SWAT team that Sam had served on. He took Sam's death hard with the bonus of guilt because he hadn't been able to save his best friend and brother-in-law. Rory and Sam had been inseparable as kids, and both joined the police force after college. They moved up the ranks to the elite SWAT team together, and Rory led the raid in which they were surprisingly outgunned. Rory had been wounded but Sam was fatally shot. She knew he blamed himself for not being able to save Sam, no matter how many times she tried to convince him otherwise. Rory was responsible to a fault. She never would have thought to blame him, but he couldn't seem to not blame himself. Police work was the family business. Their father and uncles were all cops, and they grew up hearing how dangerous it was. Her brothers and Sam had idolized their father and followed in his footsteps to join the D.C. Metro Police, but when they lost Sam, it changed all of them.

"Actually, my boss mentioned a job in New York. I was thinking I might apply," she said, testing out the idea on him.

"That's a big move, and you should absolutely apply," Rory said with a lopsided grin that pushed a dimple into his cheek.

"You don't think it's too crazy?" she asked.

"No. Hell, I'd consider leaving too if I wasn't so entrenched here."

Charlotte laughed. "The golden son would never leave. Mom and Dad would be devastated if you moved away." She punched his arm. "The price you pay for being so dependable."

"You should tell them you're considering the opportunity. Let them warm up to the idea."

"I will. I just need to find the right moment."

Rory shoved her playfully. "Get changed, I wanna see how bad we'll beat you in this relay before I spark up the grill."

"At least give me Finn, to make it a little more challenging for you."

"You must be crazy. I plan to swim on my back, because I'm counting on our little brother's swimming skills to carry the load."

"We never stood a chance," Charlotte whined as Rory exited her room.

An hour later she lay on a lounge chair wrapped in a towel trying to warm up in the last remnants of sun next to Finn. Her heart still pounded from the relay race; meanwhile her youngest and toughest brother looked like he'd barely broken a sweat.

"You could at least pretend to be a bit worn out from that race and the freezing water," Charlotte said.

"Child's play." Finn's deep voice was muffled by the hat covering his face.

Rolling her head over to look at him she spotted a new

tattoo on his right shoulder.

She poked the intricate sword and his shoulder muscle flexed. As a Navy SEAL, he was in exceptional shape. She imagined all they did was work out and shoot guns between missions.

"Are you joining a biker gang? Every time I see you there's more ink on your arms."

"Nah, it was my parting gift from the guys."

Charlotte knew better than to make a big deal out of any information she could pull from her very serious little brother. Of the four Maguire kids, Finn was the most introverted and intense, which said a lot if someone got to know Rory's controlled demeanor. She was born after Rory and the only girl. Conner was referred to as the middle child due to his extroverted and sometimes immature tendencies. Charlotte had been outgoing before Sam was killed, but death can sober a person to the realities of life.

"So, you decided not to re-up your time in the military? Dad mentioned it was time for you to decide again."

He moved the hat from his face before answering. "Nope, I'm done after this tour. Mom and Dad don't need that stress. Not after losing Sam." Finn reached out and squeezed her hand. She wasn't surprised by the display of comfort as much as his declaration of leaving the military, but she played it cool.

"What's next, kindergarten teacher? Barista? Maybe a gap year living abroad," she teased.

"Law school or the police academy."

"Out of the frying pan into the fire?"

Finn laughed. "I'm only cut out for a few things in this

life."

"Ain't that the truth," Conner said, pulling up a chair and setting a cold beer on Finn's eight-pack abs. "Charlotte, is it true you're looking to move away?"

She sat up on her elbows astonished that he'd heard about her grand plan already.

Conner was the charismatic loudmouth who rounded out the family and somehow always knew everyone's business.

Finn eyed her and gave a low whistle. "Mom and Dad are going to love that."

"Maybe your news will help lessen the blow," Charlotte said.

"So, it's true?" Conner said, pulling off his shirt to catch the fading sun.

"Maybe. There's a job in New York with my firm I could apply for, but nothing is set in stone. I still have to be selected."

"New York?" Conner and Finn said in unison.

"I'm not sure about living in that dirty, noisy city permanently, but it's a great opportunity to move up in my company," she said, smoothing her beach towel out beneath her.

"I mean I agree your OCD tendencies might go off the rails, but they probably have loads of hand sanitizer," Conner said. "Does this job come with a promotion?"

"Being organized and liking starch is not the same as OCD, look it up," Charlotte said.

Finn scoffed, and they both waited for Charlotte to answer the question.

"Technically yes, it would be a new role in the company, as the director of global marketing."

"Isn't New York the mecca for all things PR and marketing?" Finn asked. "Sounds like an easy decision."

"As long as you're going for the right reasons, I don't see how you can turn down the job," Conner said.

Charlotte appreciated her brothers' support. Now she just needed to get the job. Part of her was terrified to move away from home, while the other part was excited for the chance to reinvent herself. It was one thing to travel three hundred days of the year, but quite another to leave for good. Her family was her support system, even when she kept them at arm's length, she knew they were just a short drive away. In Virginia, she was always going to be Sam's widow, but in New York she could be anyone.

Chapter Two

AFTER THE WEEKEND with her family, a new PR project was just the escape Charlotte needed. The lake and all the police shop talk with her dad and brothers still reminded her of Sam. Even though she knew they tried to limit it when she was around, police work was in their blood, just like it had been in Sam's. Monday morning, she woke up and drove straight to the airport in Alexandria to catch a flight for her latest assignment in Canada. It was a seven-hour flight, so she forfeited spending the holiday with her family to be in place at the glamorous hotel in downtown Vancouver for a Tuesday morning start. Usually, she spent her flights plotting PR and marketing plans, but thoughts of Sam kept popping into her mind. They'd planned to live in Alexandria—where they both grew up—to raise kids and grow old together. Now he was gone, and she was going to rewrite all their plans.

Once she checked into her hotel room, she ordered room service and spent the night finalizing her plans for her current project, a premier Cavalier hotel in the heart of Vancouver. As a leading boutique hotel company with international reach, Cavalier was a trendsetter in the industry. Her job was to get a bead on the local area and create an advertising blitz that would fill the hotel restaurant, spa, and bar with local traffic by the time it opened. PR and marketing were always done at the end of the project, and in this case, she had two weeks.

Charlotte spent the first two days learning how the city flowed, where the locals and tourists liked to concentrate their time. Did the hotel have easy access to public transportation? Would the convention center feed a large amount of traffic to the hotel and its amenities? She scheduled advertisements on popular local radio and morning news shows and used the new Cavalier hotel business suite to work in between trips to scope out the city. On her third day, she made a point to arrive by seven a.m. to get a head start in the quiet office space before the other team leads arrived.

Once her computer powered up, she grabbed her mug and water bottle to fill in the staff kitchenette. Deep in thought, she exited with her full coffee and water, running smack into a thick, broad chest. Two strong hands steadied her while holding onto her elbows with a gentle grip, but she felt their heat. If only she'd glanced up a moment sooner, she would have had an extra second to compose herself. Instead, her heart sank to her stomach when she looked up to find Caleb Kincaid a breath away, looking down at her with dark, brooding eyes. The one man in the company she avoided like the plague.

"Caleb, you're in Canada?" she said.

His reflexes saved him from getting coffee poured down his suit, but some of the hot liquid sloshed out of the lid onto her hand, causing her to wince.

"I mean hello." She cringed trying to shake the hot droplets off her hand without spilling more.

Dropping his hands from her elbows once she steadied herself, he produced a handkerchief from inside his breast pocket—the perfect gentleman with a half-smile that spread across his handsome face causing her heart to pound against her will. Her hands trembled, and she hoped he didn't notice. Unfortunately for her, Caleb was the type of man it was impossible to ignore.

"Good morning, Charlotte. It's nice to see you again," Caleb said.

His husky voice reminded her of how early in the morning it was. An image of him in bed invaded her mind followed by instant mortification. Caleb looked polished for the day in his well-tailored suit and a freshly shaved jaw. His light brown skin looked permanently kissed by the sun, and his thick dark locks were still damp from a morning shower. The man's good looks were a menace, and from the smile spreading across his face, he knew it. Embarrassment caused her cheeks to burn hot as she recalled what a flirt she'd been the first time they'd worked together.

She knew she should say something, anything, but felt mute under his watchful eyes.

"I've been in town for a couple of days, but city fire codes and permits have been consuming all my time. I was pleased to see you'd be leading PR on this project," Caleb said.

She couldn't help but notice the way his athletic build filled out his suit. He hadn't changed a bit, still gorgeous and intimidating. A fresh wave of guilt deepened her blush and even her scalp felt hot. She knew she shouldn't feel anything for Caleb. It was a betrayal to Sam's memory, but her thoughts weren't her own when it came to him.

She took a deep breath and itched to smooth down her always wild hair, but her hands were full.

"I trust you have everything under control?" he asked.

His tone was professional with a hint of uncertainty as he carried the awkward exchange.

She knew he was the new VP of East Coast Endeavors now but that didn't explain why he was working on this project. Standing there dumbfounded, she could only guess what Caleb must be thinking of her lack of professionalism.

Finally, she found her voice. "I didn't realize you would be on this project. I mean, weren't you recently promoted to a VP position?" She fumbled.

She clung to the idea that he wasn't working on the same project as her for the next two weeks.

"Correct, but I managed a previous opening in Vancouver last year, and the Canadians can be prickly. Management asked me to handle this opening before my promotion was announced. Here I am."

"Oh." It was all she could muster as the shock rolled over her. If he was managing this project, that meant she would be forced to work with him and report to him. Two weeks of torture.

His scent wafted around her while he studied her in silence as if he didn't recognize her. They both stood staring at each other for a moment before he spoke.

"You've had a couple of days to get the lay of the land. I'd like to hear your promotional plans for the final advertising push soon, once you're ready."

"I have my rough draft, which I hope to solidify after a few more meetings today."

Moving out of her way, he let her pass him before he walked toward the coffee machine.

"Let's meet tomorrow morning if that works with your schedule," he said over his shoulder as he made a cup of coffee.

He was politely ignoring how flustered she was. Meanwhile, he wasn't even fazed by seeing her. He probably had this effect on women all the time and was accustomed to ignoring it.

"Perfect, I'll coordinate with your assistant."

He nodded in agreement, and she turned to walk away relieved but annoyed with his unaffected manner.

If she didn't know better, she could swear Caleb's eyes followed her as she retreated, but she didn't dare glance back to see. She had a full day of interviews with local media outlets to publicize the new hotel and needed to get her mind right.

Sitting back at her desk, memories of the first and last time she'd worked with Caleb flooded her mind. It was the first time they'd met, on a month-long project in Rome. She didn't speak any Italian and the project turned out to be far more complicated than she expected. Lucky for her the manager on the project, Caleb, spoke perfect Italian and agreed to help her. He was the type of man that wore his good looks like an afterthought, and Charlotte wasn't immune.

They spent almost every day together: working lunches, exploring the city, and constructing advertisements in

English and Italian. At the time she was still dating Sam. As the boy who lived next door, then her first serious relationship, it was hard for her to remember a time when Sam wasn't in her life. Charlotte always thought of Sam as hers, and by the time she was in high school, her crush was borderline obsessive. But Sam was a senior when she was a freshman and didn't pay her any notice. When she got to college at 18, it was a different story. Of course, her brother Rory despised it, but he conceded he would rather see his little sister with one of his friends than some other random college student. They dated off and on for the next five years until Charlotte had the opportunity to travel to Rome. Sam encouraged her to sow her wild oats, not thinking she actually might.

Caleb had just moved to Rome after being relocated for their company. She played tourist as he learned his new surroundings. Admittedly she flirted shamelessly because she knew it couldn't go anywhere, but it all came to a crashing halt on her last night in Rome. Caleb walked her back to her hotel after a celebratory dinner and he kissed her. She immediately understood the error of her ways when the touch of his lush mouth evoked red hot desire. With her back pressed against her hotel room door, she came to her senses moments before things went too far.

After abruptly ending the kiss, she explained she wasn't interested in a one-night stand and didn't mean to mislead him. He said it didn't have to be one night. But she knew there was no point in entertaining the idea of starting something with Caleb when they lived an ocean apart. She could still recall the look of disappointment in Caleb's eyes when she said she was already seeing someone. It wasn't a proud moment for her, and she'd avoided any future projects in Europe. Seeing him again, the five years that had passed felt like five minutes.

×

CALEB FOUGHT THE urge to ask Charlotte how she was truly doing after everything she had been through in the last few years. Her curves were leaner, and her eyes looked less dazzling than when he'd met her five years ago, but otherwise, she was the same intoxicating beauty. Thick auburn hair she used to wear in long waves was pulled back, hazel eyes with flecks of green and gold showed her emotions as plainly as her blushes. Touching her had been unavoidable when she came barreling out of the kitchenette, and her familiar vanilla scent greeted him like an old friend.

He sipped his coffee, staring out the large window in his makeshift office of the new hotel. It seemed ludicrous that he ever thought he wouldn't be affected by her, even after so much time had passed. The last time he saw her she'd welcomed his mouth on hers as their bodies molded to each other and he held her in his arms. Then she destroyed him right before they both lost control. Her confession that she wasn't single and wasn't interested in a long-distance hookup had been like a sucker punch to the gut. After accepting a dream job in Europe, he'd met a woman he didn't want to let go of and she was already taken. He told himself it was his mind playing tricks on him. That his connection to her was because he'd just moved halfway around the world. But his grandmother's words haunted him. "When you meet someone you cannot forget, you'll know she is the one".

Their chemistry was a lifetime ago, and now he was the VP in charge of East Coast projects; he couldn't afford to get distracted by a pretty face from his past. They'd gone their separate ways, but fate was taunting him by putting her in his path again.

His thoughts were interrupted by his phone ringing, and his sister's picture flashed on the screen, giving him a warning of who called.

"Katie, what's up?" he said in greeting.

"Oh good, you're not blowing me off again. I wanted you to know I'll be in Vancouver in time for dinner."

"Tonight, why?" Caleb worried something must be wrong.

"Because you're my big brother and I haven't seen you in a year and flying to Vancouver from Seattle is shorter than a flight to New York."

Caleb let out a deep breath. "Fine, but you'll have to meet me at the hotel. I have a tasting menu for the hotel restaurant tonight."

"Great, see you at seven." She hung up before he could respond.

He never should've confided in Katie about his abnormal scans in Italy. She'd badgered him tirelessly to see another doctor ever since. One pitfall of childhood cancer meant annual tests to make sure it never returned. In September his Italian doctor called him in for a second round of blood work after his first test indicated an anomaly. He had every intention of following up with a specialist in Rome, but when Cavalier decided to promote him to VP and bring him back to New York, he got busy. The move had been hectic, and he didn't feel sick, but the Italian doctor had felt certain there was something amiss with his tests. Now he had to balance a new job that required a lot of travel with more doctors' tests. He didn't need to get distracted by Charlotte Maguire James. For some reason even saying her married name, felt like swallowing nails.

Chapter Three

"CHARLOTTE, PLEASE TRY this and tell me exactly what you taste," a familiar voice demanded.

Looking up from her work, she found her friend and head chef, Marco, holding a baby blue plate. He placed the delicate setting down in front of her followed by a dramatic flip of a napkin he set on her lap. Marco was by far the most temperamental team member she'd ever worked with and her closest friend within the company. Each new Cavalier hotel required a team to bring the boutique style and modern elegance together before the hotels opened. They had worked on dozens of projects together over the years, and he was also the only person to never treat her with kid gloves after Sam died. He called her his food muse and would force her to try new dishes he created for hotel openings or go out into whichever city they were working in to try the local food.

Now her mouth watered as she studied the stylish plate in front of her.

"Beautiful presentation," Charlotte said.

Three bite-size scallops on top of petite circular pieces of toasted brown bread, with a drizzle of a bright orange sauce fanned out like a flower on each scallop. Before she could be annoyed with his interruption, her stomach growled. She plucked a scallop off the plate and popped the entire bite into her mouth. Closing her eyes while she chewed, she held back any reaction, gaining a grunt from Marco.

"Well?" he said.

His impatience was amusing, but she took her time to consider the flavors exploding in her mouth.

"I smell saffron, hmmm…" The buttery warmth of an expertly seasoned scallop burst in her mouth. She liked to see if she could trump Marco in his test of her taste buds.

"Pepper, cumin, salt, and is that lavender, or am I imagining it?" Charlotte asked.

She licked her lips and opened her eyes to see Marco smiling proudly. Several feet behind him stood Caleb intently watching her with an appreciative smile before his jaw flexed. Her throat constricted, and she began to cough from the intensity in Caleb's stare.

Marco tsked and handed her the water bottle on her desk.

"Too much spice?" he asked.

"No, it's perfect." She made a point to look only at Marco as she slowly drank her water.

"I call them Marco's saffron-kissed lavender scallops. Spectacular, right? Couldn't you just eat a dozen of those?"

She couldn't help but laugh at Marco's pompous attitude toward his food. He personified the stereotype that chefs were snobby about food.

"Impressive taste buds, Charlotte," Marco said over his shoulder as he walked away.

Caleb was in the team office speaking with one of her

colleagues, and while her desire to avoid him was cowardly, the compulsion to run was strong. She needed to pack up her things, but looking down at the remaining scallops, she couldn't resist eating them. Rushing from one meeting with the radio station that afternoon to several other media outlets, she'd forgotten to eat lunch. Polishing off the last scallop, she stood to gather her things.

"It sounds like you have a keen sense of taste," Caleb said.

She didn't notice his approach until it was too late to escape. His height forced her to look up into his espresso brown eyes shrouded in long lashes. It was impossible to stop her body's reaction to his nearness. Butterflies in her stomach, sweaty palms, followed by embarrassment, she felt like a schoolgirl with a naughty crush. Hoping he would leave without speaking to her again was futile.

"Marco always makes me try the dishes he develops for his menus. He says he likes to see how someone with an untrained palate finds the food," she explained.

Caleb's laugh was deep like a bass drum and sent shivers over her skin while her stomach dipped with awareness. Her breath caught in her throat and her skin tingled. An early evening shadow ran along his jaw that she had an intense urge to touch. Either her body was having a heightened reaction to him, or he had this effect on every woman. She hadn't thought about touching a man for two years until now.

"Every time I do an opening with Marco, I gain a few pounds from the tastings. But I can understand him wanting a sounding board for the menu, and I appreciate his diligence," Caleb said.

He glanced around the busy office and seemed unaware of her reaction to his nearness. Numerous account leads and their assistants remained later than normal, likely waiting for Caleb to depart. Even Marco lingered while chatting with the pretty interior designer.

"Excuse me," Caleb said as he moved away from her, as quickly as he had appeared.

She was relieved to end their odd exchange yet disappointed at the same time. She didn't like how her body was on high alert around him. It was as if he turned on a light she hadn't realized went out.

Caleb's voice rose above the chatter in the office space. It took her a moment to understand what he was saying because she was so distracted by his nonchalance toward her and how good his butt looked in his slacks. He was corporate eye candy.

"I know it's getting late so I'll be brief. I just received word from the CEO that he needs to move the final presentations up a few days to Monday. That shortens your prep time to fine-tune your accounts, but everyone seems to be on schedule. I'd still like to do a run-through with each team lead by Saturday. Please speak with my assistant to get on the schedule. Thanks, everyone."

Caleb delivered the news with a kind tone but the expectation to complete each aspect of the opening, a week early, was clear. Everyone accepted his update with professional grace. Before he departed the office she watched as several women batted their eyes at him. They didn't even try to hide their flirtation, and she couldn't blame them. He was too gorgeous for any woman to ignore.

Once he was gone, several of the hotel staff grumbled about not having the necessary equipment yet to do their jobs, but the show must go on. Her promotional content was ready to go live once Caleb approved all the advertising spots she planned.

Most of the team had planned to spend the weekend seeing the sights, but now they would need the time to tighten up their accounts. Each hotel opening was complete after the executive manager, in this case, Caleb, reviewed every element. Then the CEO was briefed on everything, and he gave the final approval on the completion of a project and all the marketing she developed to be launched. Charlotte would have the new hotel added to the company website for reservations, advertisements on all major search engines, social media presence launched, and local ads for the restaurant, spa, and event rooms.

Grabbing her bag, she shoved her planner and laptop inside before she walked to the kitchen to return the plate and thank Marco. When she walked through the ornate doors into the chic restaurant, the lights were dimmed. The room had remained unused, but tonight she found a beautifully adorned table for two in the middle of the dining room with candlelight. Caleb stood with his back to her as he looked out a large window at the city lights. It was like her thoughts conjured him standing across from her. In reality, it was obvious he had plans to dine with someone.

Clearing her throat to make her presence known she felt like an idiot interrupting him.

"Right on time," he said but stopped short when he

turned and saw her standing in the doorway.

"I was on my way to return this plate and thank Marco... Wait, on time for what?" she asked.

Before he could respond, a curvy woman with light brown skin and bronze highlighted hair walked into the restaurant, smiling at Caleb, right before she threw herself into his arms. Charlotte quickly made a beeline for the kitchen before she had to witness anymore. There was no denying his excitement at seeing the other woman or her own disappointment.

Charlotte stood against the kitchen door, her chest heaving as she tried to catch her breath. The last thing she wanted to do was crash Caleb's date night. For a split second in the dining room, she thought he was waiting for her. She let her mind wander—about what it would be like to enjoy his company before she snapped back to reality. How was it possible she was still affected by him all these years later?

Five-year-old memories of Caleb's touch and their sexy make out, played over in her mind. She could still recall how turned on she had been when his hand had moved to grip her neck before his mouth enveloped hers. He'd been intoxicating as he took control of the moment, and she'd clung to him as he pushed her against her hotel room door. Caleb had been the complete opposite to Sam and every man in her family. The men she grew up with were clean-cut alpha males who worked out hard and only dressed up when forced. Caleb made an expensive suit look casual, and his dark waves of hair were long enough to run her fingers through. Thinking about it again was disrespectful to Sam, but Caleb invaded her thoughts all day.

"Charlotte, why are you lurking in my kitchen? You never come in here, least of all when I'm cooking," Marco hollered over the open fire of the grill where he was searing something.

She pushed away from the kitchen door and tried to relax her tight shoulders.

"You told me to return my plate." Moving quickly, she placed the dish in a large sink and stalked toward the back entrance. "Have fun cooking for the boss. His date just arrived." She couldn't hide the distaste in her voice after seeing Caleb with the woman.

"Charlotte," Marco called with a playful tone, "that my dear is the supply closet. If you want the back door, it's the other one with the glowing red exit sign above it. The French call it the exit." Marco nodded his head toward the opposite direction she was walking. "It'll take you to the main lobby near the service elevators. Or you can stay to watch a master chef in action, and I'll feed you too." His tone was playful and probing.

She turned to face him with a smile while gritting her teeth.

"Thanks, but I planned to get a run in before dinner. The scallops were delicious. Thanks for letting me sample them." She knew the best way to distract him was to talk about his food.

"If I were allowed one critique, I'd say less cumin and maybe add a different ingredient for heat. It'll give it that spice I think you're looking for to balance the buttery flavor of the scallop and the floral lavender tones." She smiled sweetly, then crossed the kitchen to the exit door.

"Watching the Food Network doesn't substitute for culinary expertise, but maybe I'll try your suggestion, smartypants!" Marco called after her.

Charlotte laughed as she walked down the stairs to the lobby. Catching a cab a block away, she made her way back to her hotel. As night enveloped the city she wondered where Caleb was staying, then winced at the idea of him taking his gorgeous date back to his room. She needed to focus on the project and impress Caleb enough for him to vote for her promotion, not worry about his dating life.

WATCHING CHARLOTTE STALK off when his sister arrived put Caleb in a dark mood for dinner. Sitting in the opulent restaurant with a view of the harbor, finally seeing his sister for the first time in a year, and all he could think about was Charlotte. He had only been in New York for a week before he was sent to Vancouver for this final project and had too much going on with work to be distracted by a woman who had already rejected him once. But thinking of all the logical reasons not to be interested in her didn't help.

About halfway through their first course, Katie called him out on it.

"Look, I know I sorta sprung my visit on you, but you could at least pretend to have missed me in the last year since I saw you in Florence."

"I'm sorry, you're right. I'm feeling a bit out of my depth," he confided.

"Is it the new job, the move, or both?"

"Both, and neither. I mean the job will be challenging but I'm confident I can master it. And I'm relieved to be living in New York again."

"So it's a woman. The only reason you're ever grumpy is over a woman. It seems funny I didn't figure this out sooner, but you haven't talked about anyone special."

"There is no one, special or otherwise."

Katie looked around the modern French-themed restaurant humming, "mmmhmm."

"Who was the woman you were talking to when I walked in?"

Caleb narrowed his eyes. "Just a colleague."

"Huh, it seemed like more. It seemed like she was eager to get away from you."

"Maybe I would have figured that out if you weren't on time for the first time in your life."

"Touchy. Did I interrupt something?" Katie teased.

"No, unfortunately." He cringed at the disappointment he felt.

"She is very pretty," Katie said. "She has a sort of ethereal, yet conservative vibe. I bet she's wild when she lets her hair down."

He fought the urge to smile and poured her another glass of champagne. "How is Seattle?" he asked, hoping to change the subject. The last thing he needed to wonder about was Charlotte's wild side.

"So, who is she?" His little sister was like a dog with a bone, and she wasn't going to drop the subject.

"One of my colleagues. I haven't seen her in years." He ran his hand over the white tablecloth thinking back to the time he spent with Charlotte in Rome. "I made a mistake the last time we worked together, and she's probably worried I'll hit on her again." He took a long pull on his glass.

"Now this is getting good." Katie tipped her glass. "How do you know it was a mistake? Did she reject you?"

"In a way. She married someone else."

"Ouch." Katie fiddled with her glass. "Maybe she just couldn't pick up and move her life to Rome."

"Yeah, it was a longshot."

"Is she still married?"

Caleb laughed. "You like to sniff out all the clues. You should have been a lawyer instead of a reporter."

Katie smiled and leaned across the table. "She's single again and now you both live in New York?"

"Not quite, she's widowed and lives in Virginia."

Katie slapped the table causing their plates and glassware to vibrate.

"So you've got a chance."

"No. I'm currently her boss, and we live several states apart. Besides, who said I'm still interested."

"Oh, you're interested and it's ruining our meal, so just accept it and figure out how you're going to win her over."

Shaking his head, he couldn't help but be amused by Katie's optimism.

"I don't think she would be interested in any kind of romantic relationship, and I'm not interested in making a fool of myself."

Katie frowned. "If you have a connection with her, you need to go for it."

"Here I thought we were going to have a nice quiet meal

and you were going to bore me talking about some stud you're dating."

"Oh, we can do that next, once you promise you won't write off the universe giving you a second chance with the one that got away," Katie said.

"So, you're a hopeless romantic now. What's his name?"

"Who?"

"The man that made my driven sister sound like a greeting card on Valentine's Day," he said.

They both laughed. "His name is Dr. Joseph, he is gorgeous, treats me like a princess, and I think he might be the one."

"Now that's big news."

Caleb refilled both their glasses. "To finding the one and proving Nonna was right."

"To my big brother's promotion and moving home."

"Cheers." He smiled at his sister's contagious mirth.

"Now tell me how you're going to win the widow's heart," Katie said.

Caleb groaned. "I should never have told you."

Chapter Four

THE NEXT MORNING Charlotte dressed in her favorite navy-blue suit with a cheerful pink blouse. She arrived at her usual time and queued up her presentation in one of the conference rooms. For the next hour, she rehearsed her marketing campaign to brief Caleb, then reviewed emails. There was a note from Renee confirming the new marketing position in New York being advertised, and an overwhelming urge to apply filled her. She pushed it aside; she needed to get through this meeting first.

"Hey doll, I bet you skipped breakfast," Marco said as he walked in carrying a tray stacked with plates, and a pot of coffee.

"Didn't your mom ever tell you being a know-it-all is annoying?" she said. Teasing Marco was always fun.

"Yes, in fact, she did, but then I already knew that, as a know-it-all," Marco said.

"I walked right into that one."

"Listen, if you're briefing Caleb this morning that means your account is ready to rock and you know my kitchen is in order, so I'm taking you out tonight. There's this great salsa restaurant nearby on the water."

"I hope you mean chips and salsa because I don't dance.

I'll embarrass us both."

"That could be fun too. Come on, we'll drink margaritas surrounded by strangers. It'll be great."

"Fine, I don't have the energy to argue today. What did you bring to bribe me with?" She lifted one of the shiny silver lids off of the plates now set at the head of the table.

"That's Caleb's breakfast, but I won't tell if you eat it."

"Too late," Caleb said, appearing in the doorway.

Charlotte dropped the lid, cringing as it clattered down.

Her cheeks heated.

One second in the room with Caleb and she was already blushing.

"Oh, that color looks nice on you, Char. What do you call it, blush?" Marco said. "Don't worry I made you one too because I knew Caleb wouldn't want to share."

Charlotte caught Caleb watching her as she took in the conference table now set for two.

"Enjoy," Marco called over his shoulder before he exited.

"Thanks, Marco," Caleb said, never taking his attention off of her. "Good morning. Please have a seat."

His tone was commanding, and her knees wobbled. She stood still wondering if he was this bossy in every aspect of his life. He wore a light gray suit that draped expertly along every inch of his muscular frame, and she was spellbound.

"I hope you don't mind, but I asked Marco to provide us breakfast since I'll have back-to-back briefings. I'm a little early so we can eat first and then run through your promos." Caleb stood, waiting for her to take her seat.

"Oh, I ate already."

She could hear the nervousness in her tone. Panic raked

her mind at the idea of having to share a meal with him while making casual conversation.

Caleb narrowed his eyes, challenging her lie, and she squirmed under his scrutiny.

"Alright, I guess I could eat more. He does make the most amazing butter croissants," Charlotte conceded and sat.

Caleb lifted the coffee pot to pour them each a cup before he took his seat.

They were both quiet as they uncovered their plates. The silence began to feel like a standoff, but she knew she should break first. Nailing her marketing pitch was easy. Making small talk with her sexy boss over an unexpected breakfast was not.

Blowing on her coffee, she watched as he took a few bites of his expertly prepared omelet. Sipping the piping hot brew warmed her, and she clutched her cup like a lifeline.

"I heard you're on a shortlist for a promotion in New York," Caleb said between bites.

She nearly sprayed him with her coffee from the shock that he knew she was considering the move. Gulping down the hot sip she had just taken, she coughed into her napkin as he leaned forward and patted her back like a child. His warm hand soothed her through her blouse and blazer.

Mortification flooded her. Knowing her face was bright red, she hoped he thought it was from her choking.

"Was that supposed to be a secret?" Caleb asked.

"No," she said, dabbing at her watery eyes. "It's just that I only found out about the position a few days ago."

His large hand enveloped his coffee cup, and his eyes studied her as he sipped.

"On my first day in New York, the head of marketing tracked me down to tell me she planned to poach you from the field team. She wants you to take over the new global marketing position in her office." He paused for another sip. "I support your promotion if you want to progress your career in that way and move. You've built a strong reputation with your unique PR skills, but the corporate side can be less creative."

"I appreciate that, but I think it's the best next move for me." She was unsure where this conversation was going.

Caleb flexed his hand on the table before speaking. "Charlotte, I want to make sure you aren't uncomfortable working with me. I realize in your current position your work falls under my management chain." He fiddled with his fork, but his eyes remained focused on her as he continued, "I need to be sure you aren't pursuing a new position because you want to avoid me?"

She gulped her coffee again, unable to break eye contact as the hot brew rolled down her throat.

His chiseled features were stern, but his eyes hinted at a vulnerability. Too distracted by how his teeth ran over his bottom lip she forgot to respond.

"I was unprofessional in Rome when we worked together. I never should have kissed you. More importantly, I should have made a point to apologize if I offended you," Caleb said.

His brow was furrowed, and his full lips folded into a grimace.

It was clear he regretted kissing her. All this time she had held that moment on a pedestal, and he wished it had never happened. Finally, she found her voice.

"There is no need to apologize. The project in Rome was over when we kissed, and you were never unprofessional. If anyone should apologize, it's me for sending you the wrong signals."

A soft smile broke on his face that looked forced, and he shook his head.

"I'm not uncomfortable working for you. I want the job in New York for a change of scenery and to advance my career, not to avoid you."

"Good." He smiled as if he'd won some battle that she didn't know they were having.

She looked away from him to straighten the silverware next to her plate and searched her mind for a new topic. In desperation, she grabbed a croissant off the plate and took a big bite. The buttery moist delicacy melted in her mouth, forcing an involuntary groan.

Caleb's eyes met hers and grew darker before a mischievous smile touched his lips. He plucked a croissant off the plate and took an equally big bite. They both chewed, staring at each other.

"Irresistible," she said once she finished her mouthful with a forced laugh.

He nodded.

From the way he was looking at her, and the butterflies at war in her chest, she didn't think either of them was still talking about the delicate pastry. Was he toying with her after practically retroactively rejecting her five years ago? Charlotte took another big gulp of her coffee and glanced at her watch.

"Alright, in the interest of time, why don't you eat and I'll get started with my presentation." Charlotte stood and brushed the crumbs off her dark pants. Her nerves were completely shot after five minutes with him. There was no way she could function if she had to work with him on every project in the field.

✕

THE STRUGGLE NOT to reach out and touch Charlotte was overwhelming. She seemed on edge around him. He had to assume she felt the same electric vibe between them, but she clearly wanted to ignore it. He knew it was the professional and gentlemanly thing to follow her lead, but he couldn't force it to go away. Even after all this time she was familiar to him, like they'd been doing this dance around their mutual attraction for years.

Instead of enjoying some time together, she grabbed the remote for the slides like a lifeline and began her spiel. The opportunity to study her while she spoke was too good to pass up and he couldn't help but enjoy the view. Today her amber-hued hair hung in big waves over her shoulders. He could see the outline of her trim waist and long legs in her suit. She barreled on, outlining her three areas of concentration for the new hotel's marketing blitz. Pulling up the social media, she noted the high number of hits and interest in the spa and bar. Finally, she provided a breakdown of every advertisement that needed his approval, and each outlet they would market starting that weekend.

"I approve of all the advertisements; you've obviously

mastered the local market. Marco told me they already have reservations booked a month out due to the buzz you've created," he said. She was impressive, to say the least, and the deep red of her cheeks indicated she was humble about how good she was at her job.

Sitting back in his chair, he read the last slide with her logo for the social media sites.

"Let the day fade into a delicious night."

"Very good," he said before standing. He could sense a change in her mood. She had been nervous to brief him, but now that it was over, she could relax.

"Renee and the New York office will be lucky to have you. Once you get the promotion we won't work together directly, but I may need to pick your brain on projects from time to time."

"I won't mind," she said but pressed her lips together.

Part of him still wondered if she wanted the job in New York to avoid working with him, because he didn't believe for a minute, she'd sent him the wrong signals in Rome. He could feel the tension between them even now; desire pulsed under their professional facades. He was tempted to test her resistance even though it was unprofessional.

"I'm glad things aren't awkward between us," he said, challenging her to speak up if she disagreed.

"I'll just go fire off these ads now that you've seen them," she said, looking away and gathering her things haphazardly.

"We have a little time if you want to finish your breakfast," he offered, gesturing to her untouched omelet.

"I'm good but thank you. I'll see about having our dishes cleared before your next meeting," she offered as she made her way to the double door exit.

Initially, he'd convinced himself their connection was nothing more than lust after she'd rejected him in Rome. When he'd heard she married someone else, he had no choice but to push away his disappointment and move on. But fate had made her single again, and after being around her for two days it was clear they had unfinished business.

✕

THE DAY FLEW by and before Charlotte knew it, she had a margarita in her hand while listening to the Spanish band at a breezy seaside bar. She was exhausted from the nerves she'd had leading up to briefing Caleb, but it was Friday and she could relax.

"This place is amazing, yet completely unexpected here," she said to Marco over the music.

"I know. Stick with me, kid." Marco did a hip shake to the beat of the music. "Let's dance."

"No way. I don't know how to salsa, or tango, nothing but a country line dance."

"Then you won't mind if I find another dance partner," he said while scanning the bar for a prospective target. "Cal can keep you company."

She turned to find Caleb striding toward them at the bar. He was dressed casually in jeans, a gray T-shirt, and a light coat. A mix of desire and raw nerves sent a shiver down her arms and her stomach sank. His eyes ran over her and lingered. She pulled on her blazer feeling overdressed in the suit she'd worn all day. Her heartbeat pounded faster as he stopped to stand next to her.

"I'm glad you could join us, Cal. Can you order another round? I'm going to try to convince someone to dance with me. Charlotte claims she has two left feet," Marco said.

He was gone before she realized what he was saying, and Caleb hailed the bartender's attention to order three more margaritas.

"You look like a deer caught in the headlights." He smiled. "I take it Marco didn't mention he invited me."

Pulling out a chair that opened at the bar next to her, their elbows touched, sending a wave of heat up her arm before he picked up a drink and set it in front of her.

"No, it must've slipped his mind," she said.

He picked up another drink and clinked it to hers while she watched as his tongue tasted the salted rim. Desire forced her thighs to squeeze together as he took a long sip of the margarita before facing her. His eyes sparkled, and she realized she was gawking at him.

Breaking eye contact, she gulped her water as several of their colleagues from the hotel project arrived; the women were excited to see Caleb. She listened as they complimented his casual attire and management style. He was gracious with a touch of formality that made it clear he wasn't interested in flirting.

"Would you care to dance?" the young perky interior designer asked him.

"I'm afraid I have two left feet like Charlotte," Caleb said.

She suspected he was lying and that he was good at dancing. His forearms flexed as he fiddled with his drink, and she forced her eyes to look away.

"We're going to find a few willing dance partners," another of the local staff hired for the hotel said, nodding to a group of men across the bar from them.

"Do you really have two left feet?" Charlotte asked once the women were gone.

"Care to find out?"

"Oh no, I actually would trip over my own feet or yours, not to mention our eager colleagues would probably take me out."

Caleb's deep laughter filled the space between them, and she couldn't help but smile.

"You're underestimating my skill to lead you but you're right. It would probably look bad. Especially after I turned down the others."

"Obligations of being the boss," she offered and sipped her drink again. The tequila expertly hidden in the lime and tang of the margarita was working its way through her limbs, forcing her body to relax.

They sat in quiet companionship at the bar, watching strangers dance. She was at a loss of what to do. Her instinct was to run but her reflexes were numb, and her thoughts were shot down by her body's desire to stay close to him. In the crowded bar, it was impossible to keep much personal space. Her arm continued to brush his as they took turns sipping their drinks, and she enjoyed the warmth of his body heat so close to hers.

"Did you find a place in New York easily?" she asked.

"I did." He turned his body to face her before continuing, "The real estate scene moves fast, so when you find something you like, you just have to go for it. The company has a firm they recommend, and after I gave them some basic parameters, they did the rest."

She felt his eyes on her, but she didn't meet them. Instead, she watched a young couple walk onto the dance floor and begin to move in sync in a choreographed dance they must have practiced a million times.

"The tango is the dance for lovers," Caleb said as the woman's blue skirt swished around her knees.

"I can see why. It's amazing how connected they appear." She found Marco's lean form twirling a woman with dark features out on the dance floor too. She hoped her usually pale skin looked less severe under the soft bar lighting.

"Looks like Marco found a formidable dance partner," Caleb said.

"You sound like you'd like to be out there too. Don't let me stop you from enjoying the venue."

"I'm enjoying it just fine sitting here with you."

She met his eyes but was unsure what he was thinking; she couldn't read him at all. If she took him at his word, he was content to sit with her and have surface chit-chat over dancing with one of the gorgeous women eyeing him since he'd walked in.

"I think I should go. The margarita was stronger than I expected." She stood and slipped her purse over her shoulder.

Caleb nodded with a forced grin marring his handsome face. She itched to smooth the lines along his forehead.

She placed her hand on his arm before she realized what happened, and his eyes met hers. The warmth of his bare skin under her palm ran through her but the disappointment in his eyes felt like a blow to the gut.

"You don't seem like the kind of man to sit in the shadows when there are so many beautiful women just hoping to get your attention."

She intended to sound playful, but her voice sounded forlorn in the noisy bar.

"I'm not sure you know what kind of man I am, but I'll warn you I am a very patient man."

The implication was he wanted something more from her, and she didn't think she was ready to hear what was on his mind.

"Good night, Caleb."

"Good night." He stood like a gentleman before she walked away.

She wasn't used to the chivalry he exuded; it was the polar opposite to the humble courtesy the men in her life usually paid her. Her relationship with Sam had been built on years of friendship, and they shared a familiarity that came with knowing each other for two decades.

Exiting the bar without a look back was difficult. She couldn't help but feel the magnetic attraction to Caleb still there after all this time. Maybe it wasn't specifically him; maybe her hibernating libido was waking up again and reacting to being around a virile, attractive man. Some men were too intoxicating, and he was one of them. The attraction was raw and overwhelming, but she wasn't ready for all the emotions he stirred in her. It was clear she couldn't work with him regularly. Her nerves couldn't take it.

Chapter Five

"*C*HARLOTTE WE'RE GOING *to be late if you don't shake a leg!" Sam called from the hall.*

Looking in the mirror, she took a deep breath and smoothed her peach linen dress. Why was this material so difficult to wear? Why did it always wrinkle so fast? Why did she choose this dress for today? Getting engaged was way too big an event to happen with chipped nail polish and a wrinkled dress.

"Babe, come on," Sam called.

"Coming." Charlotte charged out to the living room, expecting him to be waiting by the door impatiently holding their luggage. They were headed to the lake house for a romantic weekend away and Sam had been acting weird.

Instead, he was kneeling in the middle of their living room with rose petals scattered around him. The lights weren't dimmed and there was no music, just Sam with his gorgeous smile, bright blue eyes, and sandy blond hair.

"Charlotte Marie Maguire, will you marry me and make me the happiest man ever?"

Charlotte's hands trembled as they covered her mouth. Her feet moved as if she was a puppet on a string.

"Okay babe, this is where you can talk." Sam reached for her and pulled her to sit on his one knee. "Are you really

surprised or is this you freaking out? It looks like you might be freaking out, like the time you were twelve and broke your hand. Did your life just flash in front of you?

Charlotte nodded. No one knew her better than Sam. He knew all her secrets, her worries, and desires. As the literal boy next door, their courtship was an inevitable conclusion, and she always knew they would end up together. Ever since she returned from her trip to Rome, she'd sensed a shift in their relationship. So why was she so hesitant now when he was offering her exactly what she wanted?

"Babe?"

"Yes, of course, I'll marry you. I thought you'd never ask." *Sam kissed her, wrapping her in his arms, his mouth hungry on hers.*

"I love you, Char. I promise I'll spend my entire life making you happy."

Charlotte woke up with a start under a weighted blanket in her familiar bedroom. She reached her arm toward the empty side of the bed where Sam once slept and used to hog the covers. The blanket lay perfectly tucked and there was no dent in his pillow. Sam had been gone for two years, but every morning there was a moment when she remembered. It used to feel like a bucket of cold water was being dumped over her head. Now it was just part of her routine.

A minute later her alarm went off, and like a robot, she got out of bed to dress for a run. Every morning for the last year she ran. It started as a way to quiet the voice in her head, a form of meditation where she could block out everything going on in her life and was forced to breathe.

Now it was a habit she was afraid to break. Little things she could control in life comforted her because life was so unpredictable.

After a day of trying to get in touch with Renee to discuss the position in New York, Charlotte started to second guess her impulse to apply for the job. Then she was informed by the scheduling department that she was being assigned to the opening of a new luxury resort in Southern Virginia, effective immediately. The Pinnacle Resort would be the largest project she ever developed PR for and would normally take weeks. A junior marketing team member had started the project but failed to hit the sales markers expected. They needed Charlotte to fix it. She typically avoided projects in Virginia because she liked to travel farther away from home. But this resort was an almost two-hour drive into wine country, so hopefully, it would feel far enough. She didn't need to analyze why she liked to travel so much for work; she knew she was avoiding home. Just like running, it was a coping mechanism developed out of necessity after Sam died. If she was focused on work outside of town, then she couldn't be focused on Sam's absence.

Finally, Renee called her back as she started to pack.

"Hi, I've been trying to reach you. I wanted to talk to you about the job in New York, but I just found out I was assigned to the Pinnacle Resort."

Renee interrupted her before she could finish her awkward attempt to ask if she was passed over for the New York position.

"I was hoping to talk to you before scheduling told you, but everything happened so fast. The CEO believes if you can fix this mess, it will demonstrate the scope of your skills."

"So it's a test?"

"Basically. If you successfully market the resort, the job in New York is yours," Renee said.

"No pressure at all."

This made the job in New York very real, and her palms started to sweat.

Renee laughed. "You're exceptional at PR and marketing, but we had several applicants from outside the company with a lot of experience. Luckily, management would prefer to hire from within. So just rock this project like any other and you get New York."

"Right, like any other large-scale resort, weeks behind on promotion, no problem." She paused, gathering her thoughts not wanting to sound unprofessional.

"I have complete faith in you, but remember you'll have extra eyes on you. Ciao." Renee hung up.

Charlotte thought about the prospect of moving to New York. The job was hers for the taking or losing. Anxiety about living in such a big, bustling city washed over her but then Caleb popped into her mind. Working in the same city as him would be easier than working for him. There were 8.3 million people in New York. She wouldn't need to worry about one intimidating, gorgeous man.

The following day after an almost three-hour drive due to several pit stops for coffee and pictures of the scenery, Charlotte stepped out of her car to breathe in the country air. Located in the foothills of Shenandoah Mountain surrounded by rows of grapevines the Pinnacle Resort stood out like a sprawling grand country estate. Charlotte took a deep breath that caught in her chest when she spotted a row of geese in the lake to the left of the main building.

Late-afternoon sun reflected off the water, casting a golden glow over the property. Grabbing her bag, she walked toward the majestic stairs leading up to the wide plank wood porch accented by white rocking chairs. The double doors looked at least ten feet tall and heavy with metal handles in a braid pattern. Before she could reach the doors, they opened inward via a sensor. Stepping into the lobby, the country chic vibe ramped up with rustic chandeliers, supple leather chairs, a large fireplace to the right, and gleaming herringbone-patterned wood floors. The smell of cinnamon hung in the air.

"Wow," Charlotte said, taking in the ambiance.

"You must be Ms. James," a woman at the front desk said, breaking Charlotte's mental checklist on how to showcase the resort in promotional photos for her PR push.

"Hi, I was told to arrive before five to make sure someone would be available to give me a room key," Charlotte said.

"I appreciate you making it in time. The opening staff are all staying on the first floor." The woman pointed to the right of the fireplace and slid a key across the marble counter. "We're still training the housekeeping staff, but there is always someone around if you need anything."

"Thank you." Charlotte accepted the key and made her way down the first-floor hallway with vivid black and white prints of a vineyard hanging on the walls. She opened the last door on the left, and the plush aesthetic of her room caused her to practically purr. A large four-poster bed sat opposite a wall of windows letting in the sunshine through gauzy white curtains. A thick gold and green rug accented the light wood floors in a cozy sitting area next to a gas fireplace. The view of the garden maze and mountains in the distance was impressive.

She was intimidated to be brought in at the last minute on such a large project, but it wouldn't be a hardship staying in this fancy room.

Chapter Six

T HE FLOOR WAS cold on Caleb's bare feet, and a draft wafted in the back of his paper-thin gown. Back in New York, he was finally following up on his abnormal blood tests in Italy the month before.

"They really should make different sizes in these things," Caleb grumbled as he sat on the paper-covered table while the nurse typed notes in a computer on wheels.

The elderly woman's fingers floated over the keys quickly, and he wondered how much information she could have possibly found to write.

"You certainly are in good shape. That will work to your advantage."

Caleb nodded, waiting for her to tell him he was in perfect health, but she didn't even glance his way.

"The doctor will be in to speak with you," she said, setting her icy blue eyes on him. "We won't know anything, Mr. Kincaid, until your blood tests and body scans come back."

"I was hoping for a clean bill of health," he said.

The nurse smiled and her bright-pink-painted lips parted to show perfectly straight teeth. "Of course you are."

Just then a middle-aged woman in a doctor's coat walked

in. "Good morning, Mr. Kincaid, let's have a look at your file."

The nurse exited.

An hour later, he'd had blood drawn, a full-body scan, an x-ray of his previous cancer site, and a referral to another specialist. The doctor insisted he needed to follow up with the dermatologist right away while waiting for the blood test results. There was a spot on his shoulder she didn't like the look of. After getting dressed, he shoved his tie in his suit pocket antsy to get away from the medical suite.

His phone began to ring as he approached the subway tunnel, and Katie's face flashed on the screen. He'd told her he had the appointment set so she would stop bugging him about it, but it seemed to be having the opposite effect.

"They won't know anything for a few weeks," he texted, not wanting to miss the next train. He'd been out of the office longer than he expected, but being short with his sister wasn't going to help. "Stop worrying. I feel great," he added, hoping to appease her.

"I'm here if you need me," she fired back.

Stowing his phone, he made his way down the stairs to the train platform. He hadn't lied to his sister, but he hadn't told her everything. He did feel healthy, but a foreboding had settled over him when the doctor said he needed to see a dermatologist about the spot on his shoulder. He didn't need a medical degree to know it wasn't a good sign. Memories of hospital rooms, stiff bedding, needles, and his parents' worried faces flooded back. When he was a kid, a routine check-up after falling out of a tree resulted in a cancer diagnosis. A week later he had a kidney removed. He missed three months of school, and everyone had treated him like he'd hit the lottery because he beat cancer. His dad referred to him as his lucky charm ever since. Even though his doctor said the type of cancer he'd had as a kid wouldn't spread to his skin, he couldn't help but think something was wrong. He had to pray his luck would hold.

He didn't have time to be sick; this new VP position required every ounce of his focus. He oversaw every project on the east coast of America and needed to get a better handle on which new hotels weren't meeting milestones. He already identified one problem child in Virginia. The Pinnacle Resort was supposed to be Cavalier's new flagship venue and should have been given more attention leading up to the grand opening scheduled for the end of the month. The marketing suffered when a junior staff member got in over their head and quit the firm. He requested Charlotte take over the project because he trusted her work, which gave him two reasons to visit the site in person.

Chapter Seven

NEARING THE END of her first week revamping the Pinnacle marketing plan, Charlotte accomplished a lot. She set up several new social media sites and spent hours populating them with photos she had taken by a local photographer. Her vision to marry the luxury of the resort's amenities, with the comforts of the laid-back country lifestyle was coming together. She ate, slept, and dreamt Pinnacle Resort marketing. Renee was clear that the ball had been dropped and Charlotte needed to pick it up.

There were several other team leads staying and working at the resort but it was so massive with a vineyard, equestrian trails, an 18-hole golf course, and a full spa, they rarely saw each other. Everyone was focused on their area of expertise and knew a boss from New York would be checking in on them by the end of the week. If she had stopped to consider who was now managing all of the east coast projects, she wouldn't have been so surprised when she found Caleb in the business suite that morning.

Unfortunately, his appearance in yet another expertly fitted suit, accented by scruff along his angular jaw took her completely off guard. Her mouth dropped open at the sight of him, and her stomach buzzed with excitement. Somehow the facial hair made him look rugged and even hotter than the last time she saw him. Then her eyes shifted, and she realized he was talking to her brother Rory, who looked completely out of place in his SWAT uniform.

"For the love," Charlotte said out loud.

Both heads turned toward her as she absorbed the awkwardness of the moment.

"Rory, aren't you a little out of your jurisdiction here?" She said, forcing a smile.

"It's so nice to see you too," Rory said, walking toward her and giving her an awkward side hug. "You haven't replied to any of my calls for almost a week, then mom said she couldn't reach you, so here I am."

He was so matter-of-fact, as if every brother would drive several hours to track down their adult sibling after not hearing from them for a few days.

"I've been really busy, and the signal is terrible out here," Charlotte mumbled as she set her things down at the desk she'd claimed in the communal space.

She looked from Rory to Caleb and back. Her mind was mush.

"I was just explaining to your brother how big this project is and what a mess the marketing was until you took it over," Caleb said, shifting his dark eyes back to Rory. "Your sister is the best our company has. I'm sure she's been busy fixing the incoherent marketing plan her predecessor left," Caleb said.

She couldn't help but enjoy hearing Caleb's confidence in her or stare at him a beat too long. The project in Vancouver wrapped up a week ago and she didn't expect to see him again so soon, much less at this remote location. Her hands were clammy, and her heart was racing, yet Caleb looked relaxed and unphased to see her.

He must have found her silence amusing, because his smile reappeared and he winked as if they had a private joke, which she realized was her. She was making a fool of herself with bewilderment at seeing him.

Shaking her head, she finally found her words, "Mr. Kincaid, I didn't expect to see you on this project," she said.

"Ms. James," Caleb said with the hint of a smirk at her formality in front of her brother. "There are a lot of eyes focused on this project, but I'll fill you in later. Enjoy some time with your brother. We can speak after.

"Rory, it was nice to meet you," Caleb said before he walked out of the business suite leaving them alone.

Her senses were overwhelmed with Caleb's appearance, and she wondered how long he planned to stay. How was she supposed to focus on the biggest project of her career with Caleb in such close proximity?

"Your boss is young," Rory said, jarring her back to the moment.

She had been transfixed on how Caleb's back muscles filled out his suit and deduced his tailor must spend extra time getting the fit so precisely.

"Yes, he is young for a VP. He just moved to New York, so I haven't worked with him much yet." She babbled while trying to collect her thoughts.

"He said he's known you for years," Rory said, crossing his arms as if he were questioning a suspect.

Taking a deep breath, she met his inquisitive stare.

"Why don't we get some fresh air? You can stretch your legs after the long drive and tell me why you're really here," Charlotte said and looped her arm through his. "Maybe I can get the chef to make us a snack." The best way to deflect attention was to mention food.

"You had me at snacks," Rory said and let her guide him outside.

Once they hit the crisp air Charlotte's heartbeat started to return to normal.

"Are you planning to come home for Thanksgiving next week?" Rory said without missing a beat.

Charlotte's stomach sank.

"I hadn't thought about it. This is the biggest project I've ever worked on, and I'm up for the promotion in New York."

Rory shook his head as they walked along a stone path. "You've avoided every holiday gathering since we lost Sam."

She couldn't deny it; throwing herself into her work had made it easier to put space between her and the memories of the life she lost with Sam when he died.

"Look, I get it, but I'm hosting a Friendsgiving this year. It will be a different vibe with lots of friends and less extended family."

"Mom agreed to that?" she said, slowing her pace along the path. Their mom had hosted Thanksgiving every year of her life, and it always included Sam's family who lived next door along with dozens of neighbors and family that would pass through. It was an emotional minefield for Charlotte after losing Sam.

"Mom said she liked the idea of not having to do dishes

for the week after," Rory said before stopping along the trail. "Maybe I'll put you on dish duty." He smiled but waited for her to think. "It's time to create new traditions and new memories with your family. No more avoidance."

Charlotte knew losing Sam had been hard on him too, and she appreciated his need to big brother her by always checking in on her over the last two years. He was looking out for her.

"This project is massive, and we only have two weeks left." Charlotte could tell he wasn't going to take no for an answer. She couldn't avoid enjoying life or shut people out indefinitely. "I'm not sure with the VP from New York just showing up if we'll even be off for the holiday."

Rory shrugged. "Don't be surprised if Mom and Dad drive out here with a bunch of food and force you to spend time with them."

"Well, when you put it like that…" She pushed his shoulder with hers. "I'll try, okay?"

Rory's mouth spread wide in a knowing grin, and his eyes squinted as if he knew he'd won the argument before the words were out of Charlotte's mouth.

It would be a good opportunity to see everyone in one fell swoop especially if she was going to move to New York soon.

"Then it's settled," Rory said. "Now what was that you mentioned about snacks?"

Charlotte laughed at her brother's ability to change topics so fast and never miss a chance to eat. They walked along the stone path to the main restaurant that was constructed to look like an elegant greenhouse made almost of all windows.

On the inside, the glamor dazzled.

"Woah, so this is how the other half lives," Rory commented as his eyes bounced around the large open dining room, with gold-rimmed green velvet chairs, massive globe-shaped chandeliers, and white marble tabletops.

"I know, right? It's not the worst place to work. The only problem is there isn't much in town once you're out here. Luckily the Chef has been kind enough to feed us while he's training the staff and finalizing the menu." She led Rory through the dining room toward the kitchen. There was a hallway that hid the patrons' view of the service window where food would be served once the restaurant was up and running. Standing at the edge of the counter she spotted Marco reviewing something with his staff, in the massive kitchen.

Marco spotted her and walked over.

"Charlotte, are you in trouble with the law?" Marco said.

"Very funny. This is my oldest brother, Rory."

Marco shook his hand.

"Marco is the head chef on this project and a good friend," Charlotte said, introducing them, then turning her smile on Marco. "Any new dishes you need our expert opinions on?"

"You're in luck. My team was just practicing several breakfast items. Does an omelet or eggs Benedict interest you?" Marco asked.

Rory smiled and rubbed his belly, "We will eat anything and everything."

Marco laughed. "Find a seat and we'll bring you some options with coffee."

"Thanks, Marco," Charlotte called out. They chose a table close to the kitchen to make it easy for the staff.

"This is a nice perk of the job," Rory said as a waiter set several plates of food on the table to include an array of scones and a full coffee pot. "I may visit you more often."

Charlotte enjoyed her brother's company but knew his guilt compelled him to push his way into her life more than he ever would have if Sam were still alive. Sam's absence left a gaping hole for both of them, but for Rory the guilt of being there the night Sam died and not being able to save him changed him. Not only did he carry a physical scar on his right arm from a bullet cutting through his bicep, but there were hidden emotional scars from watching his best friend die. Charlotte wasn't sure how to help her brother cope. Sam's death was a terrible convergence of lawlessness and bad luck. Sometimes the good guy died.

Lost in her thoughts she didn't realize Rory was talking to Marco until he nudged her shoulder.

"I was just asking Marco if he thought you all would have to work on Thanksgiving," Rory said before shoving a scone in his mouth.

"You know our management wouldn't expect us to all stay out here for a national holiday. That would mean I'd have to cook for everyone," Marco said.

As if on cue Caleb walked into the dining room. He strode over to their table and smiled when he caught her watching him.

"Caleb, what are you doing for Thanksgiving?" Marco asked.

Charlotte's stomach sank.

Rory eyed her but joined in.

"I'm hosting a Friendsgiving this year, but Charlotte mentioned you may need the staff to work over the holiday," Rory said, challenging Caleb before he stuck the other half of a scone in his mouth.

"No, the staff will all have the long weekend to enjoy with family," Caleb said.

"Perfect, then you're both welcome to join us in Alexandria," Rory said before grabbing another scone.

"This is great timing. I didn't want to drive to my brother's house that he shares with his five screaming children in Pennsylvania this year. But I didn't want to end up in one of those sad made-for-TV movies, spending the holiday alone with my work either." Marco stared at Charlotte accusingly.

"You're welcome to join us too, Caleb," Rory said.

Charlotte almost overpoured her coffee as she waited to hear what he would say.

"I planned to spend the day with my old college roommate in D.C." Caleb was looking at her when she glanced up. "Thank you for the invitation though."

The pounding drumbeat of her heart subsided, and she sat back to blow on her hot coffee while trying to calm down.

"We could all carpool to the area," Caleb said, looking at Marco and then back to Charlotte, daring her to say no.

Her palms began sweating and her throat went dry. Spending any amount of time, in a small space, with Caleb sounded like delicious torment.

"Sounds perfect. A chauffeur and a home-cooked meal, this is going to be a great holiday for me," Marco chimed in.

All Charlotte could do was nod and smile as panic moved up her spine. Marco excused them to give Caleb the tour of the restaurant.

"You didn't need to invite my colleagues, Rory," Charlotte huffed as he ate a third scone.

"No, but it was a good way to make sure you couldn't use work as an excuse. Now you can't skip Friendsgiving, since your colleagues are expecting to hitch a ride and get a hot meal."

"Micromanager," she said, yanking the last scone off the plate and taking a big bite.

Rory frowned. "I don't know what you mean. I just visited to check on my little sister's wellbeing and extended a friendly invitation in case they didn't have anyone to spend Thanksgiving with." Leaning back with a full belly, he sipped his coffee.

"It was nice of you to drive out here. I hope you weren't too worried."

"Are you kidding? This is the best meal I've had in months."

"You should work less and then maybe find someone who likes to cook since you love to eat so much." Charlotte surveyed the nearly empty plates on the table.

"Not a bad idea," Rory said, before finishing his coffee and pushing back his chair. "I'm going to find the little boys' room, and then I better head back to the city. I have a shift this afternoon," Rory said.

Charlotte carried their plates back to the service window and caught another glimpse of Caleb while Marco was talking to him with his hands flailing. Her skin flushed when

Caleb's eyes followed her movements, and she walked away without looking up a second time.

She found Rory back at the front doors and walked him out to his truck. Leaning down, he hugged her tight. "I'll see you Thursday," he said with confidence.

"Thanks for coming out to rescue me."

"Anytime." Rory smiled before getting into his work truck.

"Drive safe," Charlotte said.

She watched as he drove away down the majestic driveway toward the exit of the resort. A wave of sadness enveloped her as the taillights disappeared—the same foreboding that always enveloped her when it was time to say good-bye. Loneliness mixed with fear of losing someone else. She understood being distant physically and emotionally from her loved ones didn't protect her from the gut-wrenching heartbreak she would feel if she lost any of them. Nevertheless, she found it difficult not to try to protect herself.

Chapter Eight

CALEB COULD TELL Charlotte was lost in her thoughts as she walked back to the resort's main house. She didn't notice him waiting for her on the colonial-style veranda until he spoke.

"Charlotte, can we talk for a minute?" he asked.

Her head popped up, and she sunk her hands deeper into the pockets of her tan wool winter coat. The bright sun gave her auburn hair a fiery glow as it floated down around her shoulders. Sad eyes greeted him as she pressed her full lips into a thin line. She was going to be a serious distraction for the next week, but he was determined to remain professional.

Her cheeks grew rosy when she finally forced a smile and met his eyes. Taking a deep breath to get his bearings, he didn't know how to ignore the compelling attraction he felt toward her. In that moment he fought the temptation to tell her how attracted he was to her so he could see her blush again. It was unprofessional and illogical, but he wanted her.

"Are you here to make sure everything is on track?" she asked as she walked up the last step and stood in front of him.

Nodding, he ushered her to sit with him in the rocking chairs on the veranda. "There have been a few snags lately that could impact the opening. I thought it was better if I came in person to make sure nothing else slips."

Charlotte nodded. "I didn't realize how big this project was until I arrived. As the newest VP, I can understand your concern. The bosses will blame you if it's delayed."

Caleb laughed. Of course, she would understand the pressure he was under. He shrugged to let her know it wasn't the most pressing issue on his mind.

"Working with you again is a silver lining," he said, looking her in the eyes while watching her squirm a little.

"As you know the marketing overwhelmed the first person we sent, so I want to make sure you're feeling confident. If you need support I'm here to help."

Each breath caused a small puff of cold air from her lips that he wanted to capture with his mouth. She was alluring without even trying.

"I think I've made some great progress this week but I'm happy to run everything by you to make sure," she said, fiddling with her coat buttons.

"I planned to meet with each of the team leads to review their prospective accounts and see where we stand. I want to encourage the staff to leave on time for the holiday, but we'll be in crunch time after Thanksgiving. I need to know if anything is going to set back the opening at the end of the month."

"I'll get on your schedule first thing tomorrow," Charlotte said.

"Great. Let me know what you decide about carpooling next week to the D.C. area. I plan to be on the road by afternoon Wednesday afternoon."

"Okay, thanks," Charlotte hesitated as if she wanted to say more but must have decided against it. "I better get back to work. I have a few calls in with other wineries that might be interested in combining forces to lure folks out to Virginia wine country." She stood and smiled.

"See I knew you would whip this project into shape," he said standing.

She couldn't get away fast enough.

✕

AFTER GIVING CALEB a short briefing on the status of her PR account, Charlotte avoided him as much as possible leading up to Thanksgiving. By Wednesday she was unable to come up with a good reason not to carpool and figured with Marco's non-stop chattering it wouldn't be so bad. Caleb insisted on driving, and she made a point to be out front a few minutes early, hoping to climb into the backseat of his SUV for the drive. Unfortunately, Marco had the same thought and was already stretched out in the back, so she was forced to sit shotgun next to Caleb.

The first thing she noticed sitting a foot away from him was his sweet, manly scent, followed by the heightened awareness of his nearness. She could feel his body within touching distance, she could smell him, she could see the muscles of his thighs in his jeans, and strong hands on the steering wheel. Her senses were being overwhelmed with him. This was a bad idea.

"Do you mind navigating once we get closer to the city?" Caleb asked as he buckled his seat belt. "I'm not as familiar with the area, and GPS always tells me to turn after I pass the sign."

"No problem." Pulling out her phone, she tried to focus on the maps app and not his jawline covered in scruff she wanted to touch.

But he was impossible to ignore, especially when his elbow brushed hers as he leaned in closer to retrieve his phone from his back pocket. For a split second she thought he was going to eliminate the space between them and kiss her. Instead, a knowing smile spread across his face.

"I can see why people with kids have to get minivans," Caleb said, gesturing to Marco in the back. "We only have one child and he's taking up the entire backseat."

They both leaned over the console to see Marco with a sleep mask covering his eyes, a blanket, and a small travel pillow under his head as he sprawled across the seat.

"Total diva," Charlotte whispered.

"I heard that," Marco said groggily.

Caleb's smile dazzled her as they both faced forward in their seats. Smoothing her clammy hands down her skinny jeans, she kept her eyes on the road as he pulled out of the hotel parking lot. She fought the urge to watch his every move while wondering if he was still dating the gorgeous woman from Vancouver, then mentally kicked herself for being so eager to find out about his dating status. As much as she wanted to know if he was single, she didn't know what she would do with that information.

Ten minutes into the drive it was clear she'd made a huge mistake agreeing to carpool. Being this close to Caleb's visceral male presence was causing her to wonder if she would ever date again, or at the very least have sex again, and when. Those thoughts were followed by guilt heavy in her belly. She knew her attraction to Caleb was disrespectful to Sam but it was undeniable. Avoidance was her only option. As long as she concentrated on the road ahead, she couldn't get distracted by the muscles of his forearms or the pout of his lips as he maneuvered through heavy traffic.

As Marco snoozed in the backseat, Caleb drove the conversation with her. They talked amicably about binge-worthy shows and favorite places to travel. He sat relaxed and looked the part in his dark jeans paired with a long-sleeve navy ribbed shirt that hugged his chest. As hard as she tried, it was impossible not to notice his wavy dark hair, and muscular six-foot athletic build stretched out next to her. She was used to being around muscular men—it was practically a requirement in her family—but Caleb's lean form was usually wrapped in a structured suit disguising the extent of his muscle definition. Now it was obvious his body was ripped. Her thoughts weren't her own, and she wondered if he still found her attractive or what would have happened if they'd met before he accepted the assignment in Rome.

As they neared Alexandria, she took a deep breath. Relief at almost being to their destination was mixed with disappointment. The nervous attraction she felt around him played havoc on her body and mind, yet she didn't want to say good-bye.

"This was one of the more pleasant road trips I've been on," she lied.

"Good, because you're stuck with us for the return trip too," Caleb said.

Charlotte's skin pebbled with goose bumps at the thought of more time with him, but her instinct to avoid a physical attraction reared its head. The ties she had to Sam and his memory were strong. When she got married, she never considered the idea she could lose Sam; she never expected to have a strong attraction for any other man. Even though she knew as a widow she was allowed if not expected to move on, she still struggled with letting someone take Sam's place. She wasn't convinced she could care for someone or risk being so vulnerable again.

A dusting of snow started to fall just as they pulled up to her condo, and Marco finally woke up. It was agreed she would be the first to be dropped off, and then the guys were heading to their hotel a few blocks away.

"All the drives with my brothers usually involve a lot of '90s pop music and scream-singing. This was far more relaxing," she said, feeling the need to fill the space while Caleb found a parking spot.

"I'd get your bag but Prince Charming looks better cold and chivalrous." Marco gestured to Caleb before he lay back down. "See you tomorrow."

She turned toward Caleb. "I appreciate you driving and letting us tag along."

"My pleasure," he said with a mischievous look in his eyes.

She opened her door and walked to the back of the SUV, but Caleb appeared before she could attempt to open the rear door. The snow was falling in rapid fat flakes now, and one caught on his long lashes. His hand enveloped hers on her luggage before she could pull it out. The warmth and strength of his touch enticed her to move closer to him, but she fought the urge and stepped back.

"I'll carry this in for you," he said.

She moved her hand and let him take her bag.

"We better get inside; it's really coming down now," she said.

With his free hand, he lightly gripped her elbow to make sure she didn't slip on the sidewalk covered in fresh snow. A jolt of heat ran up her arm from his touch, but she didn't pull away. It was nice to enjoy his attention. He effortlessly carried her luggage in his other hand and guided her inside.

Walking through her building's lobby, she led him to stand in an alcove area out of earshot from anyone else coming and going.

Caleb set her luggage down and pulled up the handle for her.

"I hope you enjoy Thanksgiving with your friends to-morrow," she said.

Caleb's gorgeous face broke into a warm smile, his light brown eyes shined. "You can reach me on my cell if you need me, Happy Thanksgiving, Charlotte."

She nodded and smiled while her mind briefly wandered to what it would be like to need Caleb Kincaid. Instinctively she closed the space between them and reached up to hug him. As soon as she touched him, she regretted the move; he felt amazing. Better than a warm hug on a cold night, it was like finding the exact puzzle piece to fit her as his arms looped around her tight. After a few seconds of holding her breath and enjoying his warmth, she stepped back creating a less intimate distance between them. Looking up into his now darkening eyes she knew he was feeling the same desire.

"Bye," she breathed, unable to disguise the regret in her voice.

"Bye," Caleb said.

✕

"TOOK YOU LONG enough, Romeo," Marco said.

Caleb climbed back into his rental and let out a breath. "I was surprised she let me walk her inside." There was no need to mince words with Marco. He was smart enough to notice the tension between them. Checking his mirrors, he turned on the windshield wipers to push the fluffy flakes that were building up quickly.

"She's been through a lot," Marco said with a touch more concern than Caleb expected.

"I'm not looking to play the field if that's what you're worried about."

"Why don't you skip your friend's house tomorrow and spend Thanksgiving with us. You can scope out Charlotte's family. If they're crazy, it's better to figure that out early," Marco said.

"We'll see." Before he could think of an excuse to ditch his plans, the car in front of him spun out onto the sidewalk. Luckily, he had room to go around the front end still sticking out in the street, because he couldn't have stopped if he wanted to. Slamming on your brakes with the slick roads and fresh snow coming down was the worst response.

"You think we should go back to check on the people in that car? The hotel is just up there so we can walk back to help out," he suggested.

"No, they've just learned their lesson on how not to drive in the snow. Besides, it's only going to get worse out here. All these fools dumb enough to drive in this fresh powder are asking for trouble," Marco said, pointing to their turn.

"Which makes me what, a complete idiot?" Caleb said.

"The things you do for a hot chick." Marco tsked.

Caleb knew he was right, and it had already crossed his mind that he should ditch his best friend and try to spend time with Charlotte this weekend. If the snow kept up, he'd have the perfect excuse not to make the trek into the city. He already planned to stay at the hotel tonight; now he just needed to see how bad it got by morning. He'd caught Charlotte watching him several times during the two-hour drive, and he suspected she felt the same attraction to him that he felt for her. When she hugged him, it was clear she was struggling with how to act around him, and he couldn't help but hope it was because she wanted him too.

Chapter Nine

THE WEATHER CHANNEL predicted five inches before morning. Looking out the third-floor windows of her condo, Charlotte could see a blanket of snow on the sidewalks already and guessed it would be way worse than five inches. It was early in the year for so much snow but she loved it. Something about it added to the holiday spirit. After making some tea, she assessed her surroundings. It was clean and tidy but stark. There was no warmth or style to her place anymore. After Sam died, she'd packed away anything that reminded her of him, which included art they got together, sports paraphernalia he collected, pictures of trips they took together, and almost everything in the kitchen. He'd been an amateur chef and collected a lot of gadgets but when he died, she couldn't bear to look at any of it. With no reason to be home she usually managed to only stay at her place for a few weeks at a time by taking jobs that required a lot of travel.

Now she wished she'd held onto some holiday decorations or collected more personal touches of her own. Settling for lighting a few candles, she pulled out her laptop and attempted to get through her emails, but Caleb's dark eyes kept popping into her mind. She wondered if he planned to go to D.C. tonight or tomorrow morning and debated on texting him. The snow was coming down hard, and it was normal to worry about a colleague. Before she could muster the nerve, her phone chimed with a text.

Just letting you know the roads are really bad. Hopefully you didn't plan to leave your place tonight. This is Caleb by the way.

Her heart pounded and she sat up straighter.

I was just wondering how you were. Did you make it to your friend's place? she texted back quickly before she talked herself out of it. It was polite to respond, and her concern was warranted in the inclement weather.

No, there were several cars stuck in the snow on the way to the hotel. I'll regroup in the morning and see if the roads are cleared.

Good plan. She debated on extending an invitation but worried about having Caleb at a family-centric event. It was already going to be emotionally taxing for her after two years of avoiding large family gatherings.

How awkward would it be for her to show up with her hot boss who she was fighting an attraction to? Her brothers would sniff out her discomfort and then likely badger her until she spilled her guts. But she couldn't let Caleb spend the holiday alone at the hotel if he couldn't make it to his friend's place.

You can join us at Rory's if you can't get to D.C. She hit send and cringed.

I was hoping you'd say that. Three smiley faces followed.

Her cheeks warmed at the idea of Caleb wanting to spend time with her but knew it was probably just to avoid a holiday alone. She decided text was the best way to ask the question that had been tormenting her all day. Maybe if he had a girlfriend, it would be easier to pretend she wasn't attracted to him and give her brothers evidence that there was nothing between them.

Your girlfriend won't mind if you go to another woman's family holiday?

The dots of an incoming message started and stopped several times before his message finally came through.

What makes you think I have a girlfriend?

Oh, he was going to make her work for the info. She fidgeted in her seat and stood to pace as she texted back. How did she point out the woman she saw him with in Vancouver without sounding too interested?

I just assumed. People our age are usually dating someone unless you're more like Marco and allergic to relationships. She hoped that sounded playful.

I haven't dated anyone in almost a year. I'm holding out for someone special.

Her stomach flopped and her heart skipped a beat at the knowledge that he was single, but that didn't explain the woman from Vancouver who had jumped into his arms. Maybe hooking up didn't count as dating to him; maybe he was a player.

What about you? Are there going to be any guys at Friends-giving that might get jealous if I'm vying for your attention?

She gasped and her mouth fell open. Why would he want her attention? Did he mean because he wouldn't know anyone besides her and Marco, or did he mean he was interested in her? She didn't know how to respond.

I don't think so, she replied honestly.

Now I'm curious to see if you have a gaggle of followers that you've been too blind to notice.

She stared at her phone, knowing she wanted him to spend the holiday with her.

I'll see you tomorrow if you're sure you don't mind me crashing your family holiday?

All she could hear was the pounding of her heart. Their innocent texting conversation revealed Caleb was single, he wanted her attention, and he planned to ditch his friend to spend Thanksgiving with her and her family. Equal parts excitement and terror filled her at the prospect of spending more time with him while her family watched.

Marco has the address, see you there, she fired off and stared at her phone.

What was happening?

Have a good night, Caleb texted.

Good night. Charlotte texted back.

She scrolled through their short exchange, re-reading and overanalyzing while wondering how he even got her number. She assumed Marco gave it to him.

It had been almost five years since she'd met Caleb in Rome, and they'd barely had time to develop a connection back then. Not to mention she married another man, while Caleb likely had a string of gorgeous girlfriends over the years. It seemed so strange that their paths would converge again. But here they were about to spend a traditionally cozy, yummy holiday together, and she still didn't know how that happened.

The next morning Charlotte ran an extra mile in her building's gym in preparation for all the pie she planned to eat. After taking time to curl her hair and apply a little more makeup than usual, she made her way to Rory's place a few blocks away. Their parents lived in the suburbs of Alexandria, but she and Rory lived in what was called Old Town, or the original part of the city. There were quaint shops, bars, restaurants, row townhouses, and several old neighborhoods that were going through a round of gentrification. Rory probably would have been a builder if he hadn't been a cop. His home was an old, dilapidated Craftsman style house when he bought it but now it shined like a new penny.

He had a gourmet kitchen he barely used but installed for resale value and a large open concept living room with a dining room that led out to a gorgeous deck and large backyard. He set up several areas for people to sit and eat since he wasn't sure exactly how many people would attend.

Charlotte's nervous energy grew as she helped set place settings and light candles. Guests began to arrive and settled in to watch football on the huge television mounted in the living room before the casual dinner started. She was eager to see if Caleb would arrive with Marco or not. By three o'clock all her brothers, her parents, and several of Rory's police friends and teammates converged on the house. No one mentioned Sam, but she felt him with her like a familiar presence now that she was surrounded by several of his previous coworkers. She hadn't allowed her old life with Sam and her new life as a work-focused widow to collide, until now.

Her brother Conner invited not one but two women he introduced as friends, but she was happy to meet new people, people that didn't know her as Sam's widow. Caleb had yet to text her, and she hoped he wasn't stuck somewhere in the snow with no signal. Everyone was in high spirits, and she realized she hadn't told her parents yet about the job opportunity in New York when her brothers started teasing her mercilessly.

Excitement bubbled up when Marco and Caleb walked through the door, followed by panic. There were no directions on how to navigate being respectful to Sam's memory while lusting after her boss, and she didn't want anyone to be disappointed in her. She stood to greet them and felt the eyes of several people on her.

"You made it," Charlotte breathed.

"I tried to text you several times, but I think the cell towers are down." Caleb's deep voice caused her stomach to flutter, and his scruff-covered chin brushed her cheek when he gave her a quick hug in greeting. His lips were cool as he lightly kissed her heated cheek, and the contact left her blushing.

"Happy Thanksgiving," Caleb said.

The reappearance of an emotion that had been dormant for so long washed over her like a crashing wave: desire. She was a twenty-nine-year-old woman, with emotional and physical needs that she had pushed down since Sam died. Now they were raging back to life, and she was unable to squash them.

Marco elbowed Caleb. "Luckily for Cal my navigation skills are on point." He leaned down to hug her as well but cut it short when Rory walked up.

"I'm glad the snow didn't deter you from joining us," Rory said.

Caleb stretched out his hand to her brother. "Happy Thanksgiving. I hope you don't mind me crashing your day. The roads into D.C. are impossible, so walking here seemed like the safest option."

Rory eyed him but shook his hand. "Your friends must live in a more remote area. I heard the main streets were all cleared."

Caleb smiled. "I'm guessing your driving skills in the snow are far better than mine. After living in Europe with no car for several years and now New York, I know my limitations." Caleb was polite and charming, but she doubted her brother was going to warm up to him anytime soon.

"What a coincidence. Charlotte is after a job in New York," Rory said right before their mother walked up.

"Charlotte, who are your friends?" her mom asked as she took in the group.

She witnessed the moment her mom's eyes landed on Caleb and the sly smile that appeared. "Welcome to Friendsgiving." Her mom beamed.

Charlotte's nerves were rattled but she had to make the best of the situation.

"Mom, this is Caleb and Marco. We all work together for Cavalier. They're both working on the big resort project, and Rory extended an invitation when he hunted me down last week."

They both shook her mom's hand and her mom's inquisitive eyes studied them.

"Marco, you're the chef Charlotte told me about. Would you mind helping Charlotte's dad with the gravy? Otherwise we'll all be in for some lumps," her mom said as she pointed toward the kitchen.

"To the rescue," Marco said as he stalked toward the kitchen.

"Caleb, you better escape with me now. My mom's interrogation skills are far better than mine." Rory steered Caleb toward the living room where her brothers and several other men sat watching the game. Caleb cast a look over his shoulder as if he wanted to stay with her, and she looked away before he could see her blush again.

"He is quite attractive," her mother said, nudging Charlotte's elbow.

"He is a colleague, Mom, nothing more." Her voice was steady but even she heard the doubt in her tone.

"Well, by the way he looks at you, I would say he is hoping to change that."

Charlotte huffed and fidgeted with a table setting that was already perfect.

"You're allowed to enjoy his attention, Charlotte." Her mom's voice broke through her thoughts.

"I know you're right," Charlotte admitted.

"We all support you," her mom said and rubbed Charlotte's arm.

"No one talks about all the guilt that follows the grief," Charlotte said.

Fighting the tears that started to pool, she looked down not wanting to face the pity in her mom's eyes.

"No one talks about it because you shouldn't feel any guilt. You can miss Sam and enjoy your life. You can miss him and fall in love again, or dance, or just laugh. You can miss him every day for the rest of your life, but you have to live too. And living means enjoying yourself." Her mom's words made sense, but something stopped her from fully accepting them.

"Do you think Dad gets sick of you being so right all the time, or does it just make his life easier?" Charlotte said, breaking the intensity of the moment.

Her mom's glossed lips broke into a grin. "Oh, he loves it and so should you. I command you to take a big step and enjoy a day filled with new and old friends, the possibility of more, and an amazing meal. Let's be thankful for this time together."

"It is a little annoying how effortless you make it seem when you're being bossy."

"Thanks, I have worked hard on that technique. Making it seem effortless." Her mom enveloped her in the kind of hug only a mom can give. "I love you, baby girl. Happy Thanksgiving."

Turning back toward the crowd, her eyes met Caleb's again and their connection lingered like they were sharing a secret. The hair on the back of her neck stood straight up and goose bumps covered her skin.

The house was crowded with everyone visiting, and laughter and conversation bounced off the walls. The smell of roasted potatoes and baking apples mingled with the scent of cinnamon. Charlotte's dad stepped out of the kitchen in a food-smudged blue apron and stood in front of the TV to get everyone's attention. The men grumbled until he stared them down.

"We're so happy you all could join us this year for our first Maguire Family Friendsgiving." Everyone clapped and cheered. "The turkeys are done so we're going to start bringing out all the platters. Please fix your favorite drink and find a seat."

Charlotte felt her mom squeeze her hand right before Caleb walked up.

"I forgot how much I love the smell of Thanksgiving," he said as he leaned closer to her ear.

His warm breath tickled her neck.

"You two better find seats before the boys try to keep you apart," her mom said before walking over to where her brothers still sat in front of the television with the football game blasting.

"I hope my brothers weren't too intense?"

Caleb smiled. "They were too engrossed in the game to bother with me. If this table setting is any indication, we are in for a real feast today. Thank you for including me."

"You may regret that by the dessert course," she said.

"I'm ready," he said, patting his abs. "Mind if I sit with you?" he asked, placing his hand on the small of her back.

"Not at all," she gulped and moved to find a few seats still open at the table on the deck. The outdoor lights hung in a crisscross above the table, and the cool evening air felt good on her warm cheeks. There was a heat lamp in the corner, but she chose the opposite end of the table.

The candles flickered, silverware shined, glasses clinked, and Caleb pulled out a chair for her.

Once they were both settled in their seats, she worried about being able to make conversation through the entire dinner.

"I hope you didn't have to walk too far in the snow to

get here," she said.

"It was worth it."

The table was loaded to the brim with hot rolls, potato souffle, stuffing, cranberry sauce, greens, gravy, ham, and a platter of turkey. Rory stood across from Charlotte and everyone grew quiet as he said a short prayer. Then he ordered them to dig in.

"Everything looks amazing," Charlotte said to Rory.

"It's nice to all be together," Rory said, letting out a deep breath.

The din of everyone passing dishes or spooning out food onto outstretched plates created enough background noise to cover the sound of her heart pounding. Eager excitement rolled through her sitting so close to Caleb but she hoped he didn't notice her hand tremble. Marco sat nearby chatting with one of the women Conner invited and everyone else seemed to be busy talking, or eating.

"My family had this funny Thanksgiving tradition when I was a kid," Caleb said in a low voice next to her.

She could smell his crisp sweet scent, and his nearness felt like they had their own little intimate bubble, like a table for two in the middle of a busy restaurant. She leaned closer to listen and her knee brushed against his under the table.

Caleb leaned toward her, eliminating the space between them.

"We would go around the table and say what we're thankful for and give a wish for the person next to us in the coming year."

Turning to look into his eyes she wished she could read his mind.

"That's a nice tradition. What should I wish for you?" she asked. "Something you need or something you want?"

"This time of year, it's always more fun getting what you want." His smile pulled slowly at his full lips. "I can think of something we both want."

Her breath caught in her throat, and then his hand enveloped hers under the table on her lap. His warmth sent shivers up her arm. Her throat went dry, and her eyes fell to his mouth before she forced herself to look him in the eyes.

"What do you wish for us?" she asked breathlessly.

"I wish for you to get the job in New York, so you can be closer to me," Caleb said.

Searching his eyes, there was no denying what he meant. He wanted her, but it sounded like so much more than lust. She didn't dare challenge him or ask why; she knew exactly what he wanted because she wanted it too.

"Cal, your turn. What's your favorite traditional Thanksgiving food?" Marco said, interrupting them and breaking the spell.

Charlotte looked up to find almost the entire table staring at them. She realized they were going around the table to hear everyone's favorite dish. She pulled her hand from his as her cheeks heated and she looked down at her plate.

"Easy, the pie." Caleb smiled and squeezed her knee before he moved his hand away. "Your turn, Charlotte," he said.

"Same. Pie is my favorite too." She picked up her glass of wine and took a long sip.

It was startling how quickly the friction and desire between them could smolder into a raging need. She ached to hear Caleb say exactly why he wanted her to be closer in New York but knew she couldn't go down that road. She wasn't ready.

The crowd mixed well together. Everyone filled up on the traditional meal and then broke off into smaller groups to sit by the firepit or watch football. Charlotte mingled but often found herself next to Caleb or chatting in the same conversations as him. The group huddled over dessert and coffee well into the evening, and she helped play hostess as people began to leave.

Once the football game was over, she found Caleb talking to Conner.

"Do you have to work tonight?" she asked, interrupting her brother.

"Nope, I was just offering to drive Caleb and Marco back to their hotel, since they walked over." Conner smiled. "Do you want me to drop you at your place too?"

"No, I'm going to stay a bit longer and help Mom clean up."

"Conner, we accept," Marco said. "I'm not interested in walking back in twenty-degree winds."

"So dramatic," Charlotte said as Marco planted a kiss on her cheek.

"Always," Marco agreed.

Charlotte felt Conner's eyes on her as she leaned in to hug Caleb good night.

"Thank you again for having us. I'll see you Saturday for the drive back," Caleb reminded her and his hand lingered on her back.

A mix of relief and excitement washed over her at the

idea of getting to spend more time with him.

"Right, see you then." She smiled and looked from Caleb to her brother.

"Be nice, Conner." She punched her brother and walked away before he could pretend to be innocent.

It wasn't until they were gone that she began to feel the ache of missing Sam again. He was on her mind throughout the day at different points, and she kept him in her silent prayers of thanks at the dinner table but it had been a distracting day. At the same time, her mind flitted to Caleb and how nice it had been to enjoy his attention and the flutter of nerves whenever he was close by. If she couldn't be with Sam, maybe enjoying Caleb's attention wasn't so wrong.

RIDING IN CONNER'S undercover police cruiser back to the hotel was much quicker than their walk earlier that day and the roads were surprisingly clear. Conner pulled under the awning, and Caleb considered his options. He knew it was probably a hard sell, but winning over Charlotte's protective brothers seemed like a necessary step in breaking through her walls.

"Care to join us for a nightcap?" Caleb said.

Conner smiled. "Sounds great. The Scotch menu here is one of the best in town." He moved the car beyond the hotel doors and parked before they all piled out.

Marco yawned. "I'm too stuffed to drink anything more, you two enjoy. Thanks for the lift." Marco shook Conner's hand before he made a beeline for the elevators.

"And then there were two," Conner said.

The lounge was busier than he expected but there were plenty of seats along the dark wood-stained bar. He ordered them each a pour of fifty-year-old Scotch.

"I hope you get a company discount," Conner said.

After sipping the amber-hued Scotch with hints of vanilla and oak, Conner turned his head enough to eye him.

Caleb assumed bad guys buckled under Conner's intimidating stare, not to mention he was at least three inches taller and probably had twenty pounds of extra muscle on his large frame.

"So, you're interested in my sister and wondering if you stand a chance?" Conner asked.

Thumping his thumb on his glass and nodding, he met Conner's eyes. "Yes, or wondering if she's even available."

"She hasn't dated anyone since Sam died, so while she is technically single, I don't know if she is emotionally available. Losing Sam nearly destroyed her." Conner paused. "I think losing him cut Charlotte to the core on feeling too much. Coping with a loss like that isn't something a person can just get over. It stays with you. It changed her." Conner took a big gulp of his Scotch.

Caleb suspected Conner was speaking for his entire family; he'd pieced together that Charlotte's husband Sam had been a cop on Rory's SWAT team and a friend of the family since childhood.

"I can't explain it, but I've always been drawn to Charlotte. With her being single again it feels like I got a second chance but at her expense. I don't want to scare her off, but

I'm absolutely interested in dating her. Once she gets the job in New York she won't be in my chain of command, and we'll live in the same city for the first time. There won't be anything in our way."

Conner nodded. "The only person holding Charlotte back is Charlotte. I don't know how long it will take her to move beyond her grief, or if she'll ever let herself get close to someone again."

Caleb nodded.

"But it's been a long time since I've seen her smile as much as she did tonight," Conner said. "Tell me about yourself. We already know you're not intimidated to date a woman with three brothers trained to kill. What other daredevil activities are you into?"

Laughing, he accepted the warning and gave Conner the condensed version of his life.

"I was born and raised in Tarrytown, a suburb outside of New York City. I have one sister and two amazing parents. I went to NYU and started with Cavalier the year I graduated. When Cavalier opened their European office in Rome, it seemed like a great opportunity to experience more of my roots."

"You're Italian?" Conner asked.

"I'm half Black, half Italian. My dad's mom, my nonna, lived with us growing up and required we learn to speak Italian and learn to cook."

Conner laughed. "Sounds like a smart woman. It's funny how the Irish and Italians always seem to make the best couples. Our dad is Irish on both sides and Mom is Italian and Irish, so basically, they'll welcome you with open arms."

"Great, now I just have to convince your sister to," Caleb said.

Conner filled in a few blanks about Charlotte's deceased husband and how the Maguire clan were four generations of cops. Once they finished their drinks Conner shook his hand before heading home. He didn't give Caleb approval, but he didn't discourage him from pursuing Charlotte either.

That night, lying in bed he had a strong desire to text Charlotte but knew he needed to take things slow. Once she landed the job in New York he wasn't going to hold back anymore. He wanted Charlotte on several levels and after seeing the desire in her eyes tonight he was confident she wanted him too.

Chapter Ten

"*I*'M THANKFUL FOR *my beautiful wife." Sam held up his champagne flute as he toasted Charlotte on their first Thanksgiving as a newly married couple. They sat at their small kitchen table set for two, opting to spend the holiday together instead of at the usual big family event.*

"Is it cliche if we say we're thankful for each other?" she asked as she leaned over and kissed him.

"No."

The candlelight danced off Sam's blue eyes making them sparkle, and her heart swelled with love. Sam's look said everything; he desired her and loved her. She always knew exactly what he was thinking when his smile hitched up on one side.

"You have a secret?"

"Yes, and this time I managed to keep it for longer than twenty-four hours from you," he said, his eyes narrowing and his lips pursing with pride. "You honestly didn't have a clue?"

"No, now spill it," Charlotte said.

Sam pulled a folded envelope out of his back pocket and slid it across the table. He sat back and crossed his arms with cocky pride.

"You look very happy with yourself."

"Open it," Sam ordered.

Charlotte unfolded the thick white envelope and pulled out two plane tickets.

"Is this what I think it is?"

"Read it."

"Round trip flights to Jamaica, for our honeymoon? We're going?" she asked, wanting to hide the doubt in her voice.

"Yep, finally." Sam leaned closer and put his strong hand on her thigh. "You and me, a fancy room at an all-inclusive resort, sitting on the beach, five-star spa, and lots of sex, Mrs. James."

Charlotte's cheeks ached from the pull of her smile, and she leaned into a kiss that ended with her on top of Sam on the floor right there in their dining room. Kissing Sam became urgent as they began pulling each other's clothes off. Limbs tangled, lips crushed, but when Charlotte took a moment to take in Sam's bare chest muscles, it was darker than she remembered. Recognition that something was wrong struck her.

Looking up into Sam's face she found Caleb's brown searching eyes and woke up with a gasp.

"What the hell was that?" Charlotte asked, looking up at the ceiling.

Taking in the geometric gold and white curtains along one large window in her room, she remembered she was back at the Pinnacle Resort—the project she needed to focus on in order to land the job in New York.

In the days after Friendsgiving, Charlotte managed to keep her distance from Caleb and focused all her energy on the marketing campaign. Meanwhile, he announced a Christmas cocktail party for the company executives who planned to tour the resort and stay the night before the grand opening. Caleb decided they should have a party to celebrate the successful completion of the resort before it opened to the public. Each of the team leads needed to be prepared to brief the Cavalier executives and attend a celebration. They were each permitted to invite a plus one. Charlotte toiled over whether to invite one of her brothers, but she didn't want to be distracted by them. She wondered if Caleb planned to bring anyone.

In the end, she decided none of her brothers would want to attend. The Maguire men were more interested in fishing, hunting, or doing a mud run than enjoying a fancy resort. She couldn't wait for the project to be over and see if she earned the promotion in New York, but she had to grin and bear it through the presentations first.

"Relax, you've created so much buzz about the resort we're booked through Valentine's Day," Marco said as he sat next to her in the large banquet hall set up like a conference room where they waited for the Cavalier VPs to arrive.

Her breath caught in her throat as Caleb walked into the room with several well-dressed men and women trailing close behind him. After ushering the executive team to the table set across from them, Caleb stood at the head of the room dressed every bit the part of corporate eye candy. A black suit hugged his shoulders, accented by a red tie, and cufflinks at his wrists indicated he meant business. His thick hair was combed back, a fresh shave highlighted his angular jaw, and his full lips held a cocky smile. The room was riveted as he launched into the briefing of what the Pinnacle team accomplished.

Marco leaned over to whisper in her ear. "You're drooling."

"So," she whispered back as the lights dimmed and footage of the resort flashed on a large screen.

An hour later the executives all smiled as they left the conference room for a tour of the resort amenities. Later the cocktail party would close out the project. Before exiting the room Caleb stopped in front of her. "You have a big decision to make," he said.

Her heart pounded and her breath caught in her chest. "Sorry?" She didn't know what he meant.

"New York. The job is yours if you want it." His mouth lifted in a genuine smile.

"It is?" Looking down, she willed her palms to stop shaking and busied them with collecting her notes.

"You can take a little time to decide if you're still unsure," Caleb said.

His tone was gentle, and she felt his eyes on her as she studied the table beneath her hands without seeing it. New city, new apartment, new job, new Charlotte in the city that never sleeps. But it meant cutting several ties to the old life she had with Sam, selling the condo, and leaving him behind. They say you can always go home, but she knew it would never be the same. In truth, everything changed the moment she lost Sam and he had left her behind, not by choice but alone all the same. She had an opportunity to find a new path for herself or wallow in the life that was already gone.

"I don't need any more time to decide. I accept." She looked up to discover Caleb was the only one left in the room with her.

His smile faded as he studied her. "Good. Congratulations. I'll be sure to say you drove a hard bargain on negotiating your salary and demanded an office with a window." He chuckled, breaking the seriousness of the moment.

She didn't even think to ask how much the salary would be. She just knew it was an amazing opportunity to rewrite the course of her life and she couldn't let it pass her by.

"Thanks." She let out the breath she was holding and smiled up at him.

"We can celebrate at the party." Caleb checked his watch. "Cocktail hour starts in two hours. Don't be late."

"I won't," she exhaled heavily. "Thank you."

"Don't thank me. You earned this. You are the master of marketing, which means now you get even more responsibility developing the global brand."

"Sounds like I'll be busy."

"Not too busy, I hope."

✕

TWO HOURS LATER, Charlotte managed to call her parents to tell them she was accepting a job in New York and slipped on a vintage green dress she found in a local shop. Her parents were surprisingly enthusiastic about her move and assured her they would visit her in New York just enough for her not to miss them.

She made her way to the lounge off the main lobby where the cocktail hour was due to start and found the room transformed into a festive holiday party.

It was already an impressive wine bar featuring the resort's rustic glamorous style, with a glass-enclosed walk-in wine fridge and bottles of reds lining the shelves behind the bar. But now there was a large ice sculpture in the shape of a wine glass, elegant floral displays with Christmas colors, and a massive white Christmas tree decorated with red glass bulbs in the corner. Jazzy Christmas music played, forcing her to smile.

"If this doesn't get you into the holiday spirit," Marco said, handing her a martini glass garnished with a candy cane.

"Fa la la la la," Charlotte said before sipping the peppermint-chocolate concoction. "Wow."

"The drink or the bosses?" Marco said, looking beyond her shoulder to the entrance.

Charlotte's eyes found Caleb walking into the lounge with the CEO of Cavalier. He caught her staring, and she could swear his smile grew bigger. Before she could dwell on it, several colleagues joined her and Marco and the moment was lost. Everyone was excited to celebrate the completion of the project and rub elbows with the bigwigs from New York. She lost sight of Caleb in the crowd, but every time she felt eyes on her she would catch a glimpse of him across the room. The CEO congratulated her on the new position in New York before he left, and she realized most of the executives had departed for the night. By midnight the party was still going strong, and the excitement of her promotion had her wired.

Feeling a little fuzzy from the sugary martinis, she

stepped out on the balcony. The air was cold but built-in heat lamps were strategically placed to make the outdoor space usable year-round. Walking farther away from the sounds of the party, she sought solitude after a long day but discovered the hidden nook was already taken by the man that occupied every other thought she had all night, Caleb. With his back to her, she had the chance to sneak inside but instead, she walked closer like a moth to a flame.

Chapter Eleven

CALEB TURNED WITH one eyebrow arched as if he was surprised to see her, and then a sexy smile spread across his face.

"Of all the patios, in all the world you had to waltz into mine?" he said.

"*Casablanca*?"

"Gorgeous, and good taste in films." He shook his head.

"You should talk, walking around like you belong on a runway for whichever designer has figured out how to structure menswear enough to show off your physique and still look professional. Or maybe it's your tailor?"

She faltered, knowing she just revealed she had been checking him out.

"A man should at least get a dance before he gives up his tailor," Caleb said, turning the full watt of his smile on her. Music filtered out to the patio in hidden speakers and the compulsion to move closer to him was strong.

There was dark liquor in his rocks glass balanced on the ledge and he looked more relaxed than he had earlier that night.

"I'm a terrible dancer," she said.

"Maybe you just need a talented partner," he said, holding out his hand.

They both fell quiet, and the moment dragged on with Charlotte's indecision to take his hand. She wanted nothing more than to be wrapped in his arms, but that was the same reason she hesitated. Dancing in the dark seemed too tempting, but she didn't want him to walk away either. He'd kept his distance all night, but she craved his company.

"Maybe another time," she said, moving to stand next to him at the stone railing to look out at the garden. "The bosses seemed pleased with the resort before they left."

Her attempt to make small talk was weak but she didn't want him to walk away.

"They were relieved to see for themselves that the resort is complete and ready for guests." Caleb turned towards her and she watched as his eyes fell to her mouth. His hand brushed her temple as he pushed her wild hair back. "The project is over, which means I'm no longer in your chain of command. Now we're just two people with insane chemistry."

A shiver ran over her at the implication of his words, and goose bumps popped up along her arms. Taking off his suit coat, he draped it around her shoulders and let his hand linger on her back.

The smell of his sweet cologne and warmth from his body enveloped her, causing her knees to wobble. A growing desire to be close to him had her leaning in.

"Millions of people live in New York, but I'm sure we'll see each other at the office. Our work is bound to overlap at some point," she offered.

Caleb moved his hand off her back, and she could feel

him shutting her out but she wasn't ready to end the moment. She needed to test the connection she imagined between them. If she kissed him again and felt nothing, maybe she could stop wondering. Closing the space between them, she lightly kissed his plump but firm lips. His mouth opened initially in surprise but whatever he was going to say died on his lips. He took over the moment and deepened the kiss while pulling her back a few feet into a shadow beyond the lamp, where no one could see them. She knew in an instant that the attraction between them was even stronger than she remembered.

His warm hands held her face as he continued the kiss until she began to feel dizzy with the sensations that he aroused. Breathing in his manly scent as his mouth dipped lower to kiss her neck, she was lost in the sensations. She was someone new. Moving her hands up his shoulders, she wound them around his neck to pull him even closer. Her breasts pushed against his chest as he stepped one leg between hers and his hands moved to grip her hips. His intense desire matched her need for him, and their panting breaths were the only sound she could hear. He pinned her with his body against the stone railing of the balcony as their lust grew and she clinged to him. Hiking one knee up his leg she straddled his thigh as he moved it further between her legs. It was clear he wanted her just as much as she wanted him.

His mouth caressed her neck as his fingers undid the now loose pile of hair pinned back. Their hands roamed every inch of each other. She reveled in the pressure of his lips on her skin as he peppered her neck and shoulders with hot kisses. Their bodies melded together, and Charlotte risked never being able to stop. His hands slid down under her bottom to caress her while she rocked over his thigh with her ebbing need. The heat between them simmered and she wanted to rip his clothes off.

Her heart pounded in her chest, while every inch of her body tingled with expectations for what he would do next. The thought of following him back to his room lingered when suddenly an image of Sam collided with her lust.

How could she desire another man this much? She belonged to Sam for so long, yet Caleb evoked a need she struggled to deny.

Her thoughts were like a bucket of ice on her desire and she froze. When she grew stiff in his embrace, he pulled back. She watched as a wave of realization washed over him. His entire demeanor changed in a moment from openly desiring her to a cold door closing, and she couldn't even stand to look him in the eye. Before breaking all physical contact, he made sure she had the support of the stone wall behind her then stepped away.

Her arms fell to her sides and cold emptiness settled over her where the desire for him burned moments before.

He ran his hand over his face and wiped off the traces of her lipstick on his swollen lips.

"I know you're not trying to drive me crazy, that my disappointment is self-inflicted, but that doesn't make this any easier. I don't understand why I'm so drawn to you. I thought I could put it behind me five years ago. But now you're right here in front of me again, and the five years since Rome feel like five minutes." He huffed. "Every time I see you, I have to remind myself that you're not mine and you won't let yourself be."

She wanted to scream that she craved his touch, but she held back. It wasn't fair to him to voice everything she wanted and couldn't have.

Running his hand through his hair, he stood a safe distance away from her. She watched, unable to respond, knowing she couldn't give him what he needed. Finally, he slowly walked toward her.

"Unless your hesitation is due to something else? Because when I'm kissing you, and you're kissing me back, it feels like you want this too."

His body was only inches away as he placed his hands on either side of her, boxing her in. She could feel his breath on her neck as she concentrated on breathing. He was forcing her to face her feelings, but she couldn't admit out loud that he made her want more than the memories of Sam.

"I'm attracted to you, Caleb, but I can't offer you anything."

There was no sense in admitting his touch lit her body on fire with desire. Or that she couldn't stop thinking about him. Why torture them both?

×

FRUSTRATION FILLED HIM as he studied Charlotte—her swollen red lips, rapid breath, and an inability to meet his eyes.

"You can't or you won't?" Caleb said as he slowly tucked a wisp of hair along her cheek back behind her ear. His knuckles grazed her neck, and he could feel her skin tremor from his touch. But she remained unwilling to admit she wanted everything he offered.

"You won't let yourself indulge in the attraction that has been there since the moment we met?" he asked as he slid his hand over her rapid pulse along her neck.

"It's called lust," she said, but her voice cracked.

Her stubborn denial aggravated him, and he suddenly didn't want to make it easy for her to pretend there was nothing between them anymore.

"Lust." He shook his head and stepped closer before running his thumb over her bottom lip. "Maybe we're both lonely, but the attraction between us is far more than lust. You can deny it all you want but that doesn't change anything."

Her eyes glistened, proving her emotions were more involved than she would admit, and he had no choice but to push her to acknowledge the truth. He wasn't ready to give up on her. Her body swayed toward his as he dropped his hand from her skin and stepped back.

Picking up his jacket that fell from her shoulders when they began kissing, he shook it out.

"I'm not going to touch you again, not until you ask me to."

He forced a smile in response to the surprise in her eyes, then walked away. He was usually a calm man but hearing her deny the obvious attraction between them after she unraveled in his arms, broke him. Knowing she needed time to accept her feelings for him didn't help him want her less. She wasn't a conquest; she was everything he desired. but he needed her to want the connection between them. When he was close to her, his entire body was aware of her every move but he also felt her nervousness, her hesitation to take what she clearly wanted.

Chapter Twelve

RENEE PHONED THE next morning as Charlotte packed up her room.

"I wanted to congratulate you on the promotion, and discuss how soon you can be here," Renee said.

"Well, if I hit the road now, I can swing by my condo to grab a few things and be in New York by tonight," Charlotte said, only half teasing. Since finding out she got the job she was anxious to make the move.

"See, this is why I knew you would be perfect for the job."

"Thank you so much for this opportunity. I won't let you down," Charlotte said.

"Of course you won't. Look, why don't you take a day or two to get your affairs in order, and I'll secure a corporate apartment for you until you can find something more permanent. Winter isn't the best time of year to move to New York, but I promise to keep you so busy you won't notice the cold," Renee said.

Charlotte felt her smile spread across her face. She needed this. A new chapter was the right move.

"Okay, I'll see you in a few days."

"Well done on the Pinnacle," Renee said before hanging

up.

Charlotte tossed her phone into her purse and grabbed her luggage. She had a condo to pack up and sell.

Marco was waiting for her in the cozy lobby by the fire.

"Good news," Charlotte said, pasting on her smile.

"You and Caleb made up?" Marco said in a droll tone.

Charlotte's step faltered. "We aren't fighting. I got the job. I'm moving to New York."

"Of course you are. Did you think you wouldn't get the job?" Marco asked before standing to hug her. "Congrats, you can stay with me while you hunt for a place. I'm on the road so much, you won't even get on my nerves."

"Such a kind offer, but Renee said I can use a corporate apartment until I find a place."

"Even better. I hate squatters, it ruins friendships," Marco said.

Charlotte laughed and smacked Marco's arm as they walked out to their cars.

"As for Caleb, I know you two argued. He ran into me right after your fight last night, and I have to tell you he wasn't pleasant. I assume he was all wrong and you have every right to be upset, but being right won't fix it," Marco said.

"What if I'm wrong?" Charlotte asked.

"Ugh even worse, you'll have to apologize. It sucks admitting you're wrong, or so I've heard. Naturally, I'm never wrong."

"Naturally." She laughed at his idiocy.

They walked out of the majestic doors, and her next question died on her lips. "You're carpooling with Caleb back to New York?"

"Ew no, we're flying out of Dulles, silly." Marco tossed his bags in the back of Caleb's SUV before climbing in.

"Sit up front, I'm not your driver," Caleb said from the driver's seat before he caught sight of her.

"I don't see why we should both suffer on this drive," Marco said.

Charlotte couldn't help the smile that pulled at her mouth even as it went dry from the smoldering look from Caleb. His hair was rumpled, his eyes were tired, and he had the dusting of scruff along his jaw. She suspected he had difficulty falling asleep last night, too. But casual, sleep-deprived Caleb was just as hot as corporate Caleb. She felt awkward realizing they were staring at each other as Marco's head bounced back and forth between them like a ping-pong match.

"You two have a safe trip back. I'll see you in New York." She backed up and closed the door before either of them could respond.

Walking behind the SUV she moved as fast as she could in her wedge booties but heard the telltale sound of a window sliding down. Looking back, she found Caleb watching her and she stopped on the other side of the wide roadway.

"If you need anything once you get to New York, you know how to reach me," he said with a forced smile.

"Thank you." She waved like an idiot and turned to walk to her car before he could see the heat exploding in her cheeks. She could think of several things she needed Caleb for, which was why she planned to keep her distance for now.

✕

A FEW DAYS later Charlotte stood in her almost empty condo. She underestimated how unemotional she would be when her things were boxed up and she sold the condo she had shared with Sam. All of his things had been removed after he died, when it was clear she couldn't live surrounded by his clothes hanging unused in the closet. Now as she walked away from her old life, she wasn't sad, she was relieved. She'd known Sam long before they bought the small condo, and her memories of him couldn't be sold with the space.

If anything, the condo represented the worst memory of all, when her brother and father arrived that night to tell her Sam had been killed. Where she'd collapsed on the floor and required a sedative to fall asleep. Where she mourned the loss of the man she thought she would spend her life with, and where she became a woman plagued by guilt and fear of losing again. Selling the condo and moving to New York let Charlotte leave the worst parts of her life behind her, but Sam would always hold a place in her heart.

As she got her bearings in New York it was the memories of Caleb that played like a movie scene on repeat in her mind. Knowing she lived in the same city as him now made her feel closer to him. After a few nights in a corporate apartment, a unit in the same building came up for rent and she jumped on it. She had her new place by the end of her first week in the city. The cost was obscene, but it was the easiest option. The neighborhood was vibrant and busy with people in power suits and athletic gear. As long as she focused on work, she could avoid thinking about Caleb's mouth on her skin and all the other places she wished to feel it.

"Charlotte, you don't need to put in twelve-hour days. The beauty of your position is that it's new, you have no shoes to fill." Renee stood in the doorway of Charlotte's office.

Looking up from her large double monitors, Charlotte cringed, "Don't worry, I could never sustain this." Charlotte sipped her never-empty Cavalier coffee cup. "I think once the executives approve my benchmarks for the first quarter, I can relax more."

As the newly dubbed Chief of Global PR, she wanted to prove herself, so she'd spent the first week outlining her vision of how to improve Cavalier's overarching brand and marketing plan.

Renee nodded and gave her a knowing look. "So after the briefing next Friday, you promise to sleep again."

"Exactly."

"Okay, just keep it concise, provide three achievable action items like we discussed."

Charlotte walked over to the large whiteboard she requested on her first day. There were dozens of sticky notes surrounding major areas of focus she had brainstormed. It looked like a detective's crazy link chart to find a killer.

"I'm narrowing it down tonight, and I'll have a preview of the plan for you on Monday."

"I hope that doesn't mean you plan to work through the weekend," Renee said, walking into the office to study the whiteboard.

"I have some furniture deliveries tomorrow, so I can't."

Renee looked at her watch. "I better run, I've got a date," Renee said as she strutted out in her spiky red shoes. "Don't forget the company holiday party is next Friday too."

"Got it. Have a great weekend," Charlotte called before turning back to her project board. She knew it looked borderline crazy, but this was how she conceptualized her plans. Visual aids, whiteboards, sticky notes in different colors, and large graphics.

On Saturday after an early morning delivery of her new bed and couch, she mapped out a running route and then spent the rest of the weekend working. Her one-bedroom apartment had a modern open concept kitchen and living room combo, one large window that let in the morning sun, light wood floors, and freshly painted white walls. The one thousand square feet wasn't big but it was all she needed. Decorating would have to wait until after she got through the briefing. She needed to feel secure in her new role at Cavalier before she could focus on anything else in life. Updating the promotional content, creating new social media messaging, and outlining specific steps to establish a set formula for each Cavalier project was the crux of her plan. She just had to sell it to the executives.

By Monday morning she felt organized and ready to brief Renee. Her marketing plan was tailored and precise, just how she needed things. Arriving at eight a.m. usually ensured she would have the office to herself for at least an hour, but today Renee was waiting for her in her office, reading Charlotte's now streamlined whiteboard.

"You worked on this all weekend, didn't you?" Renee

pinned her with an arched brow and a pointed finger. "Don't lie."

"Yes, but my method is why you wanted me for this position. This is how I work under a deadline. I promise I'm not always like this." Charlotte set her things down at her desk as more PR team members began to arrive.

"Why is everyone so early today?" Charlotte asked.

"Our briefing was moved up. We're on at noon. So it's a good thing you spent the weekend crashing on this. A little sad, but good."

"What? Why did they move up our briefing?" Charlotte could hear her panic and tried to calm down.

"I just found out this morning. Apparently one of the partners is in town and the executives thought it was a great idea to show us off," Renee said.

"Great." Doubt washed over her. Looking at the cleaned-up whiteboard with her three prime ideas and eight outlined focus areas, Charlotte took a deep breath. "Alright, let me brief you on what we have, and we'll go from there."

Renee smiled and Charlotte swallowed her concerns.

After a few hours tweaking the plan Charlotte developed and completing a slideshow, the team made their way up to the fifteenth-floor executive boardroom. There were achievable steps to modify the currently incongruent marketing strategy, and Charlotte felt confident she could guarantee success. Renee loved it and everyone on the PR team agreed. But her confidence wavered as she stood at the front of the boardroom with her PowerPoint loaded when Caleb walked in.

"Caleb, hi," she said stupidly when his eyes met hers. She

hadn't expected him to be in the meeting. But it made complete sense as the VP for all the new hotel openings on the east coast that he would attend. His teams would be executing her PR and marketing guidelines.

Her body shivered with excitement until she took in his annoyed demeanor.

"Ms. James," Caleb said politely and looked down at his suit where she was inadvertently aiming the red dot laser pointer at his chest.

"Whoops, we're a little trigger happy this morning," Renee joked while pushing Charlotte's hand down.

There were a half dozen other account managers and executives already in the large conference room, and another half dozen staff to take notes. Everyone heard Charlotte's familiar tone with Caleb and his curt response.

He arrived projecting a sexy master of the universe vibe in his dashing charcoal suit that highlighted his muscular physique, but his full lips held no smile. Using her surname made it clear he meant all business and it annoyed the hell out of her.

Before she could dwell on it, the senior partners arrived, everyone took their seats, and all eyes turned, landing on her. Renee provided a quick overview of the new Global Marketing group's structure before introducing Charlotte and there was no more time to worry about who was in the room. It was go time and she gulped down her nerves.

"Whatever you do, don't imagine them all naked. They're distracting enough fully dressed," Renee whispered and winked at her. "You've got this."

Charlotte's mind was assailed with images of Caleb's

bronze skin and wide shoulders hovering over her. She pinched her eyes tight to push away thoughts of him naked. If there was one thing she was certain of in life, it was her attention to detail. Any briefing was easy when you mastered your topic. Meeting the powerful executives' attentive eyes, Charlotte launched into her presentation.

Ten minutes later her overview of the new Global Marketing campaign for Cavalier was complete. Somewhere along the way, it dawned on her she held an unrealistic expectation of how Caleb would treat her when she ran into him again. She assumed he would chase her, or at least attempt to get her attention. His indifference was irritating and forced her to acknowledge the fact that she wanted him to want her.

The CEO complimented her on the well-crafted marketing plan and Charlotte's vision for the company to develop a cohesive PR template. Once all the stakeholders approved of the marketing plan she outlined, the senior staff lingered for a few minutes chatting. Charlotte sipped her water and stewed over her annoyance with Caleb. It was impossible to avoid looking at him, but her irritation cooled to embarrassment.

Of course, he was cold and indifferent toward her; the last time she saw him she rejected him. He knew she had already moved to New York but he kept his distance. He was out living his life doing whatever hot, successful men did in a wild city and she couldn't blame him.

Chapter Thirteen

CALEB'S ARM ITCHED where the intravenous line jutted out of his arm to take his blood.

"How much longer is this going to take? I have a 9:30 meeting to get to," Caleb said, fighting to keep his tone calm.

As ordered by his general physician he was seeing a dermatologist who also wanted to take a blood sample and run more tests. Now as they poked him and scanned his entire body with a magnifying glass, he wondered if this was some ploy to just bill him for more tests. He'd convinced himself he was a model of good health until he'd stepped into the doctor's office.

"We're almost done, Mr. Kincaid," the doctor said, clearly not put off by his flippant tone. "We should have your results back in a few weeks. However, I'd like to do a biopsy on the spot on your right shoulder."

"Okay, whatever you think is best." He was completely distracted as his mind flitted back to Charlotte when the doctor said the spot looked "iffy" and she was going to inject a light topical numbing medication. The cold needle poked his skin, causing him to jump back to the moment.

"Damn." He flinched at the sudden pain. "How exactly

is cutting a piece of my back away a sample?" he groaned.

"It's probably nothing but we want to be extra thorough. We'll send this sample to the lab to be safe," the doctor said as she pressed a compress on his shoulder before she added a bandage.

An hour later making his way back to the office, the numbing medication had worn off and his shoulder throbbed. Stopping into a pharmacy, he noticed a flower stall and was tempted to buy a big bouquet for Charlotte, but that would probably just seem random. He kept hoping to run into her in the elevator or the lobby and planned to invite her to coffee or lunch, but he pushed down the urge. Trying to give her space as she got settled in New York was difficult. When he'd seen her for the briefing in a fitted black suit and high heels, she looked amazing and it annoyed him. He could swear every man in the room took note of Charlotte's siren-like beauty, but she appeared not to notice. She seemed happy to see him, yet she hadn't reached out to him.

She'd rather ignore their mutual attraction to stay dedicated to her deceased husband. He didn't want to be insensitive, but fate had given them another chance to explore the connection between them. She was allowed to move on, but instead was pretending she didn't feel anything.

As much as he wanted to push her into admitting she was attracted to him, he needed her to decide for herself she was ready. The lure to flirt with her and push her buttons was strong but he wanted her to admit she wanted his attention. He hoped the upcoming company holiday party would provide him a chance to break through her defenses.

His thoughts were interrupted by Marco, who let himself into his office.

"Are you bringing a date to the company party?" Marco asked as he plopped down into one of the stiff leather chairs across from Caleb's desk. "I've invited twins."

He couldn't help but laugh at Marco's audacity. "Do you think the company party is the right venue for your groupies?"

"It's not my fault the girls are so connected they do everything together, and I do mean everything," Marco said.

"Spare me the details please, and no, I'm not bringing a date."

"Still holding out for Charlotte, then? If you two haven't kissed and made up yet, I'm sure there will be gobs of mistletoe at the party."

Pushing Marco's feet off the corner of his desk, he tried to avoid his friends' mocking smile.

"We just had a disagreement," Caleb said.

"Maybe the holiday spirit will make her more agreeable. If not, you can try to talk with one of my twins," Marco said before standing. "Or you could just use the holiday spirit and the awkwardness of a company party to break through Charlotte's walls," he said before walking out.

Caleb considered the idea of pursuing Charlotte again to see how she responded. It would be difficult to ignore her all evening, and holiday parties were notorious for colleagues getting to know each other better. Why shouldn't they?

Chapter Fourteen

THE CAVALIER HOLIDAY party was a black-tie event being held at a posh restaurant adjacent to Rockefeller Center. Charlotte felt foolish walking down the sidewalk in her dark red velvet gown and hoped she wasn't too overdressed. Marco assured her the company spared no expense on the annual event and that the women would be decked out in glamorous dresses and jewels. As she walked through the lobby toward the coat check she spotted several men in tuxedos with women in long ball gowns and her tension eased.

Riding in the glass-enclosed elevator up to the twentieth floor provided a view of the ice-skating rink and grand Christmas tree. She wanted to snap a picture, but she didn't want to look like a tourist. The elevator doors opened and the harmonious sounds of Christmas carolers singing "Jingle Bells" greeted them. Anticipation and Christmas glee bubbled up in her chest when she followed the group out onto a candy cane-framed path with fake snow. A huge Christmas tree decorated in icicles commanded attention, and she stopped in her tracks to take it all in. There was a life-size gingerbread house to her right, and a Santa with elves sat on a throne surrounded by glittering wrapped presents in the middle of the room. Twinkling lights and massive snowflakes hung from the archways.

"Oh my goodness, it's a winter wonderland," she breathed. She wished she had someone to bring to the party. But the venue was already busy, and she needed to mingle to meet more of her new colleagues. What better way to do that than attending the festive holiday party solo?

Walking toward the Christmas tree, a waitress dressed in candy cane-striped tights, a green sequin dress, and pointy elf ears approached to offer her champagne. There was excitement in the air and the party was the perfect excuse to embrace some timeless Christmas traditions. While waiting in line for her turn, Charlotte couldn't help but scan the crowd to look for Caleb. She easily spied him across the room chatting with a colleague, and he was already looking her way. He held her gaze for a moment before turning away. Self-conscious in her fitted gown with a trumpet skirt, she glanced down at her thigh slightly peeking out from the slit in the fabric. When she looked back up, he was no longer there.

A few moments later there was a firm touch on her elbow.

"Eager to tell Santa what you want for Christmas?" Caleb teased. He held her gaze for an extra beat while the air crackled with the energy that always flowed between them. "You look stunning."

She fought the urge to fidget and took the opportunity to take in his expertly fitted black tux, accented by a white shirt, black silk boutonniere, and matching bow tie. He was beautiful, and an ache to lean in and smell him had her instinctively moving closer. His smile softened his gorgeous angular face making him look playful and sexy—a lethal combination. She wondered if he was reading her mind as one side of his mouth lifted into a knowing smirk and his hand moved from her elbow to the small of her back.

Forcing her eyes away from his lips, she cleared her throat. "This is quite the Christmas scene. Will there be reindeer and dancing sugar plums in the next room?" she asked.

He laughed and her skin warmed at the sound.

"If not you should put that in the suggestion box for next year," Caleb said.

He remained close to her as the line moved, and she enjoyed the feel of his heat next to her.

"What are you going to ask Santa for?"

"I'd like to know whatever happened to the pony I wanted when I was six," she said. "Will you snap a picture for me to send to my mom?" she asked before an elf escorted her to sit with Santa. Caleb and the photographer snapped her picture as she leaned in to whisper something in Santa's ear. The elf handed her a candy cane and Caleb met her on the other side of the line.

"That Santa has the best gig in town," Caleb said, showing her the picture he snapped before sending her a copy. "I planned to give you some space tonight but then you walked in looking so beautiful, I forgot."

His voice sounded husky and from the look in his eyes, she couldn't help but wonder if he wanted to say more.

"Thank you. You look very handsome yourself."

Smoothing her dress to busy her hands, she struggled to

think of something to say.

His eyes held hers as he reached out his hand to rub her arm. It was a small gesture of comfort as if to say he understood she was nervous and in uncharted waters. They stood there looking at each other for a moment before Marco appeared with two women, one on each arm and broke their spell.

"Ladies, go sit on Santa's lap for me, will you?" The women giggled as they moved to the line. "Merry Christmas, Charlotte. You look gorgeous as usual." Marco kissed her cheek and plucked a glass of champagne off a server's tray as they passed by.

"Did you bring two dates?" she asked in shock as Caleb shook his head while trying to hide a wicked grin.

"Yes, and I'm already regretting it. I should have set up my holidate agreement earlier in the season."

Charlotte looked to Caleb for a clue on what Marco was saying. "What is a holidate agreement?" she asked almost not wanting to know.

Marco rolled his eyes. "I forget you've been out of this game for years. A holidate is an established agreement with someone you find at least mildly attractive. You attend each other's work-related events and family gatherings during the holiday season, hence your holidate. No pressure to buy gifts, no strings attached, no expectations other than to not feel like a loner at all the obligatory events."

Caleb let out another hearty chuckle that made Charlotte want to get closer to him. Her reactions to him were instinctive and useless to deny.

"And this is a real thing, not just some random Marcoism?" Charlotte asked.

"Yes, it is a thing, and it would be far less work than those two are going to be tonight. Not to mention I can't take them both home for Christmas dinner. Mom would freak out." He said before downing his glass of champagne.

"Marco, I have a feeling your mom is well aware of your eccentric nature," Caleb said.

"You two should agree to terms before this party gets going. People are going to get drunk and then inappropriate behavior begins." Marco pointed to Caleb. "Trust me, don't let her out of your sight." He turned to snap a picture of the twins sitting on Santa's lap before walking away.

"As insane as Marco is, he may have a point." Caleb nodded his head behind Charlotte, and she followed his gaze to a couple making out under a large bunch of mistletoe hanging by an exit.

"Wow, I mean I'll be your Christmas party beard if you're worried about getting mauled by some of these women. You do seem to garner a lot of attention." She gestured to her right at a group of women staring at him. "They've been looking at you like a frosted cookie that they want to lick all the sprinkles off of."

Wrapping one arm around her back he gently pulled her into his side. "Why don't we check out the life-size edible gingerbread house and discuss terms."

His warm hand sent another wave of shivers over her, and she liked the idea of being attached to him for the night. An hour later as they made their way to the ballroom, she decided agreeing to hang out was just like a real date. They took turns getting each other drinks and would stop to mingle and socialize with the few colleagues they each knew, but always found their way back to each other. By midnight the gala was still in full swing as people packed the dance floor. A live band played a mix of '80s cover songs and classic Christmas favorites. The surprises continued as waiters passed through, offering candy cane martinis and chocolate truffles.

"Are you brave enough to let me guide you on the dance floor yet?" Caleb asked.

"I don't know about bravery, but I've had enough champagne and I do love this song," she admitted as a jazzy cover of "Merry Little Christmas" sounded out from the stage. Caleb led her out to the packed dance floor. One of her hands fit into his while he placed her other hand up on his shoulder. Then his hand skimmed down her arm before he spread it out warm on her back. He maintained just enough space between them for her to wish he was closer.

"Are you going back home for Christmas?" Caleb asked, looking down into her eyes and guiding her in the steps of a slow waltz.

"I haven't decided. I kind of like the idea of holing up in my new apartment and watching a bunch of Christmas movies, but then I'll miss my mom's cooking and family shenanigans. Also, I'm guessing the train ride won't be very fun with all the holiday travelers.

"The roads will be crazy, and the trains will be packed," he agreed.

"What about you? Where is your family?"

"My sister is flying in from Seattle and our parents are coming in from upstate, where I grew up. It's about an hour train ride in. It's our first holiday in New York as a family in years."

"That'll be nice. I'm sure your parents will be happy to have you both home."

"Yeah, after five years of living abroad it'll be nice. Maybe you can help me prep my apartment with some decorations. I have no idea where to start."

"Good idea. There are only two weeks until Christmas and I haven't done any Christmas shopping. You look like you could carry a lot of stuff," she said, looking from one side of his broad shoulders to the other.

"I'll carry whatever you need."

Charlotte's stomach buzzed with anticipation, and she couldn't fight the smile tugging at her lips. Flirting with him came too easily. She couldn't help but want to hang out with him outside of work, and the guise of shopping was a perfect excuse.

The song ended but he didn't let go of her completely as he led her off the dance floor. She spied the mistletoe nearby but stopped them short of the archway where it hung. He turned to face her, and she was forced to lean her head back to look up into his eyes that were daring her to make a move.

He held both her hands before sliding his palms up and down her arms then lacing his fingers through hers on one hand.

"It's late. Why don't I walk you home before either of us is scared by our colleagues' behavior," Caleb said.

"You don't have to walk me home. I'll get a taxi," Charlotte said.

"Then it won't take long," Caleb said.

They were both quiet as they coasted down to the lobby in the elevator and then collected their coats. They decided to walk a few blocks away from the tourists that converged on the area and easily found a taxi. The drive felt short, and Caleb paid the driver before she had a chance. She liked that he exited the vehicle to walk her to the door of her building.

Being with him felt so natural.

"I have a confession to make," he said, breaking the silence.

"Oh," she croaked.

"I was hoping you would contact me once you moved to town. I planned to be aloof and play hard to get."

"Oh really." She smiled but the rising tension of the truth coursed between them.

"People always want what they can't have, don't they?" he said with brutal honesty.

"Is that the appeal? You think I'm unattainable?" Charlotte asked.

"No, it's frustrating but not appealing."

She stopped in front of her building and faced him. It was freezing and the wind whipped at their cold cheeks. He met her gaze but didn't make any move. It was her turn to put herself out there, to push beyond the discomfort of the unknown and take a chance. Sparks pulsed between them, and she surprised him by moving closer. Standing on her tiptoes, she gripped the lapel of his coat in her shaking hands, closed her eyes, and lightly kissed his lips. She savored the taste of his mouth but he didn't budge. This was her move.

"Am I still appealing now?" Charlotte asked, pulling her

head back but staying close against the length of his body.

"You've never been anything but appealing to me," he said before he pulled her into him but his mouth hovered above hers.

A tidal wave of desire filled her as he finally wrapped his arms around her, eliminating any space between them. She didn't want to say the wrong thing, but he was clearly waiting for her to acknowledge what she was asking for.

"Kiss me, please," she pleaded.

His mouth enveloped hers until she moaned. After thoroughly kissing her, he unwrapped his arms from around her and took a step back. "You'd better get inside," he said with a gruff voice.

Charlotte nodded in a daze, and she turned to walk away. Before she got too far, she whipped around and called out to him, "Are you busy tomorrow?"

He turned halfway toward her with a smirk. "Nope."

"Brunch. There's a place around the corner with amazing food," she faltered.

"Okay, see you tomorrow." He started to turn away before she could change her mind, then turned back and called out to her, "Get inside, it's freezing," and watched her move for the entrance of her building.

Chapter Fifteen

T HE NEXT DAY Charlotte couldn't shake the feeling of having crossed a monumental threshold with Caleb. Something shifted, they took a step forward. There was no way to deny how attracted she was to him, and she didn't want to anymore. Even though they'd been out late, she was up by seven a.m. and had already completed a run to the park and back. She'd even been so distracted thinking about Caleb that she accidentally ran an extra mile. She wasn't sure what his expectations were for them to hang out one-on-one, and she wasn't sure what hers were. All her musings vanished when her phone vibrated on the counter. The screen read incoming video chat from Caleb, and she balked.

Her face was still red from her run, her hair was matted to her head from her runner's cap, and she didn't have any makeup on. The call stopped as she talked herself out of answering. But as soon as she set it down it started to ring again. Glancing in the embedded mirror on her closet door, she smoothed back her frizzy ponytail and hit connect.

"Good morning," she sighed.

"I know it's early, but I didn't want to risk you making other plans," Caleb said.

Her cheeks ached from smiling. "I'm new in town, remember, I don't have any plans."

"It looks like you already got a run in. How about a late breakfast and we can explore the city a bit?" Caleb asked.

"Okay." A rush of excitement at spending the day with him flooded her. She stared back at his handsome face on the phone and couldn't think of anything else to say. She was single, living in New York City, and going to spend the day with a gorgeous man that knew all her baggage.

"Great, I'll meet you at your apartment and we can walk to that place near you with food," Caleb's eyes crinkled on the sides as he teased her.

"Very funny. I'm a little rusty at this." The heat moving up her neck was disguised by her already rosy cheeks.

"It's adorable. Get ready, I'll see you in an hour."

She spied the clock in her room that read 9:30, but before she could respond he hung up.

Her smile didn't fade as she showered, anguished over which jeans to wear, and waffled between a thick sensible sweater or flowy V-neck. After blow-drying her hair, she fired off a text to Caleb.

"I'm ready."

Caleb replied fast, "Be right there."

It was a little after ten. She wondered if that meant he was on his way or he was close by already. Standing in front of the mirror in her room, she smoothed her simple soft white sweater that dipped low in front, paired with her favorite skinny blue jeans, and fashionable black boots. She hoped she was pulling off the casual and maybe a little sexy vibe. A moment later the intercom buzzed his arrival outside her building.

"Apartment 802," she said, and buzzed him in.

A minute later there was a knock at her door.

Caleb stood there with two cups of coffee in a carrier, and a leafy green plant.

"Hi," he greeted her with a big smile and a little bit of a raspy voice.

"Hi," she repeated and stared.

He was intoxicating, scruffy jaw, mussed curly hair, and playfulness in his eyes.

"This is a housewarming present," he said, handing her a leafy green plant in a white pot with fun zig-zag stripes wrapped around the bottom.

"Thank you," she said, finding her voice. "I wasn't sure if I would hear from you today." Her stomach buzzed with nerves now that he had arrived.

"No chance I was going to miss our first date." He continued to stand just outside the door with their coffee.

"Sorry, come in, come in." She stepped back and ushered him in.

His familiar scent filled the space, and she fought an urge to hug him. She didn't know how to act without the professional pretenses forcing them together. Her stomach fluttered, and her skin tingled. She was in a total state of nervous lust.

"I wasn't sure, but I put a little cream in your coffee," he said.

"Perfect."

Caleb seemed relaxed as he moved farther into the apartment and set the coffee down on the kitchen counter. After taking off his coat, he pushed up the sleeves of his T-shirt, while she watched riveted as his forearms flexed when he removed the cups from the to-go traveler. Dressed in jeans and a henley shirt that hugged his shoulders, sexy didn't do him justice. Yet he seemed unaware of how distracting his athletic physique, dark features, and full lips made him.

Trying to calm her nerves, she busied herself setting the plant on the windowsill in the living room.

Leaving the coffee on the counter, Caleb walked closer to her but stopped just shy of touching her. She could sense he was waiting for her to direct her attention to him, and she stopped fiddling with the plant to face him.

"I need to say something," he said.

"Okay." She braced herself for a serious conversation that would break their spell.

"It's been tough knowing you live in the same city and pretending it doesn't matter. I was excited to see you last night, but I didn't expect you to be receptive to my attention." He eliminated the space between them and took her trembling hands in his. "Or kiss me. I want to make sure I don't misunderstand your intentions or blow this."

"I thought you were avoiding me, or maybe lost interest. Not that I expected you to throw out the red carpet to welcome me to New York or blame you for being standoff-ish. Then last night it was so easy to just let myself enjoy your company," Charlotte said.

"I'm glad," he smiled. "But to be clear, I'm not interested in friendship. It has to be more." His tone was gentle but serious. He gave her hand a squeeze before letting it go.

Charlotte grabbed both coffees and handed him one.

"To not being friends and seeing where this goes." She tapped her cup against his.

His deep laugh caused a flutter of desire to course through her.

There was no denying she wanted to be more than friends with Caleb. She wanted to explore the connection between them that had lasted for five years. Even if it meant leaving Sam in her past.

Looking around at the stark white walls, bare wood floors, and sparse furniture, Caleb took a sip of his coffee.

"Are you a minimalist or planning to do more decorating?"

She laughed and enjoyed the lightness of the moment with him.

"At first, I was in a company unit and focused on the global marketing plan, but now I should have time to spruce up the place. I was hoping to do a little shopping this weekend." She pointed to the area where they stood by the window. "Maybe a little desk or table here. I'm not sure if there is room for much more.

He nodded. "There's a cool mobile furniture market every weekend that moves throughout the city. We can see if we can find it after brunch."

"You're going to help me shop?"

"I don't mind. It sounds better than shopping for Christmas decorations."

"Maybe we can find both," she said.

It would be nice to have someone other than her family to count on to help her with little things like hauling a rug back to her new place. Meeting his eyes, she realized the sexual tension that always existed between them, just under the surface, was in full force, especially with a bed only a dozen feet away.

"Should we try and get a table before the rush?" she asked.

He caressed her arm, causing a fissure of need to shoot through her. It was odd how a simple touch made her feel completely connected to him.

She enjoyed how he left little space between them as they walked to the local bistro. He opened doors and placed his firm hand on the small of her back when other walkers threatened to separate them. At brunch, they talked about how every city has its own vibe and the contrasts between different foreign locations they'd both visited.

"I think London is probably my favorite city of all time," she said.

"Funny, I would have guessed Rome," Caleb said.

"I did have the best tour guide in Rome and the most wonderful view from my hotel of the Colosseum," she said. It surprised her how easily they talked, and she could almost overlook how gorgeous he was if other women didn't stop to take note. But Caleb only had eyes for her through their long brunch, and the underlying electric current between them never dulled.

"It's almost one o'clock. Wanna walk off this French toast and find the market?"

She nodded and accepted his hand as he guided her out of the now very busy cafe. Once outside he didn't let go of her hand as he navigated them to the closest subway stop.

"The market is only a few stops away in a park." He said

after checking his phone. "If you find anything good, we can taxi back to your place."

"I appreciate you helping me," she said, leaning against him as they stood on the cramped train.

"I appreciate that you finally asked me out," he said as the train slowed to a stop. More people boarded at the crowded stop, and he moved his arm around her waist while pulling her back against his broad chest.

She began to feel a warm buzzing feeling in her stomach down to her toes. His warmth enveloped her, and she couldn't resist enjoying the sensations he evoked.

"I was a little worried this thing between us may have faded," he spoke into her ear as the train slowed to another stop.

"Nope," she whispered.

"This is our stop," he said with his lips pressed to her ear. He placed a kiss on her neck before gripping her hand and leading her off the train. The physical pull she felt toward him was more than attraction, but she didn't want to delve into what that meant. After exiting the metro stop, he pulled her to the edge of the sidewalk and goose bumps rose on her skin.

"I think our mutual attraction is very much alive and well," she acknowledged before reaching up to kiss him. This time she didn't hold back.

An hour later they were walking through a huge furniture market where each tent housed a different shop selling new or refurbished home goods. There were also tents filled with Christmas decorations, and she helped him select a few things for his apartment.

"I bet you didn't think you'd be stuck carrying all this back to my place today," she said.

He was carrying a large blue and green rug she picked out, rolled up, and balanced on his shoulder. In his other hand, he carried another bag full of holiday decorations.

"I'm just earning points to cash in later," he said before his full lips broke into a sexy smirk.

She was so distracted by his eyes she almost ran right into an oval whitewashed coffee table. Looking down, she studied the grain of the wood and the smoothed edges.

"The wood grain is unique," he said, reading her mind. "You have a great eye. I think I can manage both if you want it," Caleb said, watching her study the table.

"I can't expect you to carry everything back to my place, and I don't think we can haul everything on the train," Charlotte huffed. She already had two large-framed prints she purchased and a small lamp.

"Excuse me, do you have a delivery service?" Caleb asked an older woman with an apron standing close by.

"Yes, there is a minimum purchase required, and we can deliver within a five-mile radius. Do you see something you like?" The older woman pulled her worn hands from her apron.

"We'll take the table. How much more do we need to spend?" Caleb asked.

"At least another hundred and you'll meet the minimum. Have a look at our matching end tables and let me know what you decide."

The woman placed a "sold" sticker on the coffee table before she walked away to help another customer.

"You have to go for it if you love it, or the next person will swoop in and take it while you're trying to make up your mind," Caleb said.

She wondered if there was a double meaning behind his comment.

"Take a look around and see what else you like. If you don't find anything, I bet we can fit both in a taxi." He set the rug wrapped in plastic down.

Charlotte was enjoying his company while doing something so basic as browsing for home furnishings. She'd spent so much time alone over the last two years. She forgot how nice it was to have someone to bounce all these ideas off of.

Thirty minutes later they were loading the rug and coffee table into the delivery van. Charlotte ordered two barstools and a small desk that would be delivered later.

"There's probably enough room on the bench if you don't mind being close." The young man that drove the delivery truck, showed them a small space left between all the furniture piled into the back of his van. "Up to you."

"Is it safe?" Charlotte asked Caleb.

"There's a bigger tip in it if you make us your first stop," Caleb told the driver and rattled off Charlotte's address.

The young man smiled and waited for them both to climb in. Caleb sat first and pulled Charlotte to sit on his lap with one shoulder facing his chest. She placed one arm around his neck for comfort. It was as if it were natural for her to sit on his lap on any given day.

"It's fine. He won't be able to go very fast in weekend traffic," Caleb assured her.

Once the doors were closed the light dimmed, casting

them in shadows. Charlotte became keenly aware of Caleb's breath on her ear and the privacy they had since the furniture blocked the driver's seat from seeing them. They could hear the driver open and close his door and the sound of an acoustic guitar started playing from the stereo.

"This is more romantic than I expected," Caleb said before cupping her jaw in the palm of his hand.

Sparks cascaded along her skin, and she waited to feel what he would do next. His full lips captured her mouth. He was an amazing kisser. His tongue teased and coaxed her mouth open. His hand on her thigh stroked her leg through her jeans before moving up to grip her hip. There were no seat belts to keep them separated, and she moved to press her chest into his.

This was what she wanted, Caleb under her.

Chapter Sixteen

H E GROANED AS she pressed her body closer to his and his arms were around her back holding her close. His mouth was on her neck, then down to her collarbone, and she was lost in the moment. Neither of them spoke while they took turns exploring each other as they kissed. The darkness made her brave as she ran her hands through his thick hair, enjoying the opportunity to touch him. He moved his lips over her earlobe and down her throat causing her to arch her back. The sudden sound of cars honking brought her back to reality, and she gasped with surprise. His lips spread into a smile on the skin of her neck tickling her into laughter.

"Classic. So much for our intimate moment," Caleb said.

Her eyes had adjusted to the dim light, and she could see his wide grin. She leaned forward to steal another kiss.

"We're going to look guilty," she whispered.

"I don't care, do you?" he asked.

A need for more overwhelmed her. His desire for her opened the floodgates of her physical needs, ignored for too long. She moved her tongue over his upper lip and delved into the emotions swirling inside her—lust, need, and recklessness.

Caleb groaned as she arched into him.

They continued to deepen the kiss while his hands roamed up her thighs. She was mesmerized by the possibility of knowing they were headed back to her apartment. She wanted him closer but between their coats and clothes, it was impossible.

He pulled the edge of her sweater down to kiss her shoulder, then ran his tongue back up to her ear. When his mouth found hers again, she was lost in the sensations consuming her as his strong hands caressed her entire body. Her brain pulsed with desire while her skin hummed from the electric heat between them. She felt alive. Caleb's touch unraveled her nervousness about enjoying a man's touch again and made her bold enough to run her hands over his muscles, his arms, his chest, then pulling him closer with her hands up his back. Her desire overruled any sense to take things slow.

"We have to stop," he whispered in a plea. Finally, he moved his forehead to meet hers and held her face in his hands again as he breathed deeply. She caught her breath in tempo with his.

"It's like you lit a match," she whispered and hoped he didn't think she sounded childish.

"I'll make sure we don't let it burn out."

They held each other as the storm of their lust settled to a low roar. The van slowed and she could see their breath had fogged the windows. She laughed at the sight of their steam and traced a heart in the fog. She liked feeling his warmth surrounding her. It felt like he was hers to enjoy, and she kissed his neck as he wrapped his arms around her tighter. Her breath hitched as the swell of lust mixed with something new.

Once the van stopped, the dome light came on when the driver opened his door. Looking down, she found her sweater askew enough for her lacy bra to peek out.

"How quickly we unravel," Caleb said. A slightly red hue spread on his cheeks and his mouth was rosy from kissing her.

Caleb Kincaid was every bit as sexy as she imagined, maybe even more so. She hoped she could handle him when they didn't have any interruptions.

The driver knocked on the back window before opening the door.

The kid smiled and stood back, waiting for them to hop out.

She reached up and pulled her hair down, giving up on the now askew ponytail, and avoided the kid's eyes.

"We appreciate the ride," Caleb said as he unfolded from the cramped space and adjusted his clothes.

The young man seemed oblivious and started to unload their items. Caleb handed him a few twenties before grabbing the rug with one arm and the table with the other, leaving Charlotte the art, decorations, and lamp.

The young man laughed, as she watched Caleb head for the entrance to her building where a woman leaving, held the door.

He thanked the woman but didn't even notice her gawking at his strength. "Come on, woman," he called out playfully.

"Coming," she hollered back while grabbing the art and

ran after him.

"If you don't, I will, good grief," the woman said just as Charlotte passed by.

Charlotte called out a thank you over her laughter.

Inside the elevator, she tried to avoid staring into Caleb's eyes that seemed to shine with excitement, but she was transfixed. She wasn't sure what he was thinking but she hoped he wanted to pick up where they left off in the van. Allowing herself to own her attraction to him had been the first step in determining what she needed. What was missing in her life, as a young widow, as a woman.

Sexual impulses pushed aside for two years were all rising to the top. She wanted Caleb.

✕

ONCE INSIDE HER apartment, Caleb helped her unroll the new rug and set her coffee table in front of her couch.

"If you have a hammer, I can help you hang the art," he said, looking around.

He realized he was nervous about what would happen next, now that they were alone in her apartment. One perfect date and it was clear their chemistry was high, but in reality, they didn't know much about each other. When she retrieved a hammer, he could tell she was nervous too and it only made him want her more. But he needed her to be ready for more than just a physical connection.

"Can I ask you a funny question?" she said.

"Of course," he said, sitting on the couch.

"The woman in Vancouver that you had dinner with, is

she an old flame? You said you're single, but she seemed really happy to see you."

Trying not to laugh, he grabbed her hand to pull her onto his lap. "That was my sister Katie, and she was excited to see me. Is that why you wouldn't dance with me at that salsa bar? You thought I was being a player?" Leaning forward, he took in her scent before kissing her neck.

"Your sister," she repeated with an embarrassed grin.

Desire began to pulse between them, and she studied him with a seriousness he hadn't seen before.

"I have to be honest with you. I am a terrible dancer," she smiled. "But also, I don't think I was ready to be in your arms. I was sorta shell-shocked to see you again on that first project."

He lifted her back into a standing position and pulled her to stand in the small space by the window. Lifting her left hand high, he placed her other hand on his shoulder, drawing her in close to his body. Then he began to guide her in a slow dance, whispering the steps as they moved. She stumbled but he encouraged her to mirror his moves. Soon they swayed in each other's arms in step, to the sounds of the city outside and their breaths.

"I'm not a player; I don't have any old flames for you to worry about. I'm no saint but I am honest. I'm all yours for as long as you'll have me."

Looking into her eyes, he hoped the desire he saw would make her want him forever. The intensity of the moment had her clinging to him, and he could feel her heartbeat pounding. Finally ending their slow dance, he pulled her closer into an intimate hug. The kind of hug where their bodies were crushed together, along every curve and slope. He could feel her delicate hands on his neck and in his hair. He didn't want the date to end but knew it would be a mistake to move too fast.

"I'm going to say good night for now, but I'd like to take you out to dinner tomorrow or Tuesday if you're available?" His mouth made its way to her neck as he lifted her feet off the ground.

"I am available any night this week," she said before kissing him softly.

"Perfect, I'll take you out every night then. Consider it a standing invitation."

Her lips spread into a smile as they kissed and he set her back down to stand on her own two feet. Grabbing his coat, he made his way to her door. She handed him his bag of holiday decorations and he thanked her for the date.

Exiting her building, the euphoria that enveloped him was like the time he completed a marathon. Charlotte was letting him into her life, she kissed him, she wanted him. He was smiling like a crazy person at strangers as he walked down the street, which in New York, was questionable behavior, but he couldn't help it. He'd known their connection was there under the surface, but her acknowledging it made it feel more real. Now that he had the opportunity to woo her, he wanted to court her and lavish her with romance. Which even in his mind sounded ridiculous but necessary. He was going to work hard to impress her, and then they would see how well-suited they really were. It was clear their physical attraction was off the charts, but that didn't always translate into a real relationship. The most surprising part of the day was how nervous they'd both been. It reminded him of being a teenager on his first date, hoping he wouldn't screw up his first kiss.

Chapter Seventeen

"I DON'T KNOW how to dress for my date. I feel like jeans are appropriate but what if he's taking me somewhere nice? But it's a Monday and we just started dating, which means it's casual. So, I'm just going to wear jeans and that will set the tone," Charlotte spoke into the air of her cramped closet with her phone set on speaker. Conner called while she was getting ready to see what gift she picked out for their parents for Christmas, which was code for he wanted her to put his name on the card too.

"You're overthinking this," he said. "Wear jeans, they're versatile. Or you could just ask him if there's a dress code."

"I don't want to come off too stressed about what to wear. That seems high maintenance for a second date."

Conner's laugh filtered through the air, "Uh oh, second date you know what that means."

"I thought third dates were when a couple usually took things to the next level." Panic ran up her spine.

"Nope, the second date is the new third, but don't let him pressure you into anything," Conner said just as her intercom buzzed indicating Caleb was downstairs.

"Shoot he's here. I gotta go."

"Okay, have fun but don't do anything I would do,"

Conner said. "And put my name on the card for Mom and Dad's gift."

Hanging up on her brother, she buzzed Caleb up and took one last look in the full-length mirror on her wall, dark skinny jeans, brown booties, kelly-green peplum blouse, and her hair down, in as a controllable thick wave as she could manage. She swiped on a little sheer lip gloss right before she answered the door.

"Hi," she breathed as she took in Caleb's matching dark jeans and green shirt.

"Hi, we match," he laughed before leaning forward to kiss her.

Charlotte fell into the kiss like a familiar habit they'd always had instead of a new development. Being around him was comfortable and nerve-wracking all at the same time. Her skin prickled with anticipation and her heart pounded.

He ended the kiss but held her hand. "Are you ready? I made a reservation at my favorite restaurant in the city."

"Reservation, am I underdressed?"

"Not at all, you look perfect." He planted another kiss on her neck, then opened the door. "Ready?"

She grabbed a coat and her bag before she met him in the hall.

"I had a tough time focusing today," Caleb said, pulling her into his arms inside the elevator.

His kiss was hungry, and she wanted to suggest they just go back to her apartment and skip dinner. The sound of the elevator doors sliding open pulled them apart and her brain was foggy.

They stepped out onto the busy street, and the cold winter breeze pushed her hair back. Caleb gripped her hand and pulled her in the direction away from the subway stop closest to her place.

"We're walking distance to your favorite restaurant?" Charlotte asked.

"Yes, which means it will be impossible for you to ever get rid of me. I eat there at least once a week. Once you try their manicotti, so will you."

"Uh oh, we're going for Italian food? It's my weakness."

"Interesting, I'm half Italian, maybe I can be your weakness too," Caleb said, slowing down and pulling her into his arms. One hand wrapped around her back to hold her close while the other slid up her neck. His thumb stroked her chin as he studied her mouth.

"Maybe," Charlotte said breathless from the power of his attention.

Caleb kissed each side of her mouth, tasting her before he treated them both to a slow kiss, coaxing a groan from her as she clung to him.

"Get a room," a man called out on the busy sidewalk. People passed by but Charlotte was transfixed by his touch and darkening eyes on her.

"Hmmm," his lips moved from her mouth to her ear. "You've always been my weakness," he said, before moving back to her lips. One delicate kiss before he pulled away. Putting his arm around her shoulder, he guided her farther down the street until they came up to a blue and white striped awning.

"Good evening, sir. Right this way." A young man with a thick Italian accent in a white collared shirt and fitted black slacks opened the door and greeted them.

"Ciao, reservation for Kincaid," Caleb said.

The young man ushered them to follow him.

Caleb slid his arm down her back as they entered the narrow restaurant. A soft glow lit the high ceilings and clay-colored floor that wound through rustic tables. They followed the host down a narrow hallway that opened into a walled garden large enough to hold multiple tables that were spaced out for privacy. Caleb pulled out her chair before sitting across from her at the cozy table for two. There were gas-lit sconces along the brick wall, large pots with leafy plants, and a crisscross of glass bulbs hung above. The smell of fresh rosemary and basil tickled her nose, and she realized the pots were filled with herbs.

"This is lovely," she said.

The host didn't hover after showing them to their table.

"The food is even better than the ambiance," Caleb said.

"There must be hundreds of Italian restaurants in the city. How did you find this one?"

"Probably thousands, but not as authentic. My father grew up with the owner's brother."

"Ah, small world."

The host returned with water and a bottle of red wine before he departed again without a word.

"No menus?"

"Not necessary. I promise you'll like everything," Caleb said.

"How do you know what I'll like?"

"This will be my first test," he countered as he poured them each a glass of wine. Picking up his glass, he moved it close to hers. "To a delicious evening and proving I know your tastes," his mouth curved into a sexy grin.

Once the first course arrived—burrata cheese, heirloom tomatoes, fresh basil, and a hot loaf of herb-crusted bread—one taste proved she was in for an amazing culinary experience. The cheese burst with a richness in her mouth. When another waiter brought a huge antipasto dish to rival the size of the table, she decided she better pace herself.

By the final course, she cleaned her plate and was grateful she wore her stretchy skinny jeans.

"I can't eat another bite. You were right. The food is amazing and I'm going to confess now that I'll be cheating on you by coming here without you."

His deep laughter hummed between them, "I would expect nothing less. I usually sit at the bar near the kitchen and watch the chef cook while I eat. I have to warn you though. He's very charming and has a weakness for beautiful women."

Just then an older version of the host approached their table holding a small plate. Bright blue eyes met hers as she took in his debonair salt and pepper hair and weathered laugh lines.

Caleb stood. "Chef, thank you for an amazing meal. I think you helped me win points with my date."

"*Mi bella*, why haven't you been to see me before? I will cook for you, and you will forget all about him," the chef said, taking her hand in his warm, callused one, before winking at her.

Charlotte felt the heat in her cheeks from the older man's flirtatious attention.

"She was just warning me that she would be coming back without me, so you may have a chance," Caleb said.

"In that case, *bella*, these are for you to enjoy. I will see you again soon." The chef set the plate of miniature cannoli down, then narrowed his gaze at Caleb before he walked away.

Caleb laughed. "I see now that I should have opted to keep you locked in your apartment and ordered food in."

Picking up one of the miniature cannoli, she took a bite and then offered him the other half. He leaned forward and opened his mouth. She gently set the bite on his tongue and watched as he enjoyed the flavors. She studied his dark features, cat-like eyes with thick curled lashes, and his perfectly shaped full lips.

"How is it that you're still single?" she blurted out.

His smile fell a little and he laughed.

"I stayed busy in Rome with work. Dated a few women but it never amounted to anything serious. I always found a reason to end things before there was ever a question of where it was going. Mainly because I wasn't ready for anything more. I knew I wanted to return to America."

Charlotte nodded.

He leaned forward. "Do you believe in soulmates?"

"No, or I never really put much stock in it, I guess."

"I've always believed there was one woman out there for me and when I met her, I would just know," he said.

She could swear the air around them crackled, and she wished she could read his mind. Their waiter walked up, breaking their spell and set two coffees in front of them with a small box for the remaining delicate cannoli.

Caleb settled the bill while she considered his comment about soulmates. If Sam had been hers, what did that mean? Could a person have more than one soulmate? Before she could dwell on it, Caleb's hand enveloped hers.

"Let's walk that meal off." He stood and pulled out her chair as she got to her feet.

Her limbs were heavy from the wine, and she liked when he gripped her hand as he led her through the packed restaurant out to the noisy city street.

"That was wonderful, thank you."

"Food nourishes your body. Italian food feeds your soul," Caleb said.

"Oh that is good; you should work in PR," she teased.

He pulled her closer and put his arm around her. "My father cooks a lot, it's his passion, and my mom always says his favorite ingredient is love, so eating his cooking feeds her body and soul."

"That's adorable."

"My folks have always been a little over the top in the love department, but it's probably better than growing up with parents that hate each other. Although they set a high bar for my sister and me to find the right partners."

"My parents were high school sweethearts and are still happily married," she said. "Funny enough they always pushed us all to have adventures, get our education, and not settle down too soon. They might be regretting that now since none of my brothers are anywhere near getting married."

"Do you feel like you need more adventures?" Caleb asked.

"Not really. Moving to New York feels like a big adventure so far," she said.

They walked, holding hands, through a small park across from her building before finally crossing the street. A surge of excitement at the thought of him coming back to her apartment had her knees shaking. He held the door for her as they entered the foyer, and they were both quiet as they approached the elevator bank.

CALEB WAS TRYING to be a gentleman, but all he could think about all night was getting Charlotte alone. He didn't know if she was ready to invite him in, or ready for them to move into a physical relationship. But standing in the elevator staring into her glossed-over eyes, with her chest heaving, he suspected they were a foregone sexual conclusion. After unlocking the door and stepping inside, she held it open for him.

"I don't want tonight to end," she said by way of an invitation.

He walked in, closed the door, and eliminated the space between them. Taking her face in his hands to study her eyes, he struggled with the right words. He didn't want to scare her off or minimize his feelings for her.

"You get to call all the shots, which is difficult for me, but I need you to know that you're everything I want."

She smiled before sliding her hands up his chest and pushing his jacket off his shoulders. Then she unzipped her coat and let it fall to the floor.

The attraction between them was undeniable but he suspected she needed more time to accept how connected they were. Tonight he would try to show her how he felt about her.

"I'm more than ready to see exactly how strong this thing between us is," she said, pulling him farther into the apartment.

Caleb captured her mouth in his. Their fevered kisses were needy. His hands slid down the sides of her body. He felt her chilled hands tugging his shirt up to his abdomen, helping him peel it off, then watched as she studied his now bare chest. Reaching for the fabric of her blouse he pulled it up over her head. Slowly unbuttoning the material, he enjoyed the sound of her hitched breathing. Her skin pebbled with goosebumps before his hands were on her skin.

Bending forward, he picked her up and she wrapped her legs around his waist. The craving to feel her body under his was overwhelming, but they still had clothes in the way as he walked them into her bedroom.

Laying her down on the bed, he hovered above enjoying the flush in her cheeks. Her thighs were still wrapped tight around his hips and he balanced his weight on one hand above her shoulder.

"You're gorgeous," he said, moving his mouth over her collarbone.

She bucked her hips up against him.

"And distracting me from my plan to take my time. I want to savor you," he said.

"I want to devour you," she said, her voice husky.

She spread her legs wider to accommodate him while

pulling him back up to meet her mouth. He groaned with pleasure before enveloping her lips.

"You can do anything you want to me. I'm all yours, but first I need to taste you" he said.

Taking control, he pulled her jeans over her hips and off her legs in one swift motion. She practically purred as his hand stroked back up from her ankle to land between her legs. Her fingers gripped his hair as he teased his tongue around the edges of the lace fabric separating them before moving back up her body. He took his time capturing each breast in his mouth and coaxing a low growl from her.

"You're torturing me on purpose," she whispered.

He pushed back up to watch her writhe before he kneeled on the floor. She whimpered as he slowly kissed each ankle, along her shins and over her knees to land on her inner thigh. Gripping her ankles, he pulled her bottom to the edge of the bed until he was within an inch of tasting her. That was when she began to beg.

"Caleb, please," her voice began as a whisper.

He pushed his hot breath over her as he slowly climbed back up her body to lightly nibble her tender skin, he sucked and licked her neck with a smile when she begged louder.

"I've been thinking about doing this ever since I saw you again, maybe ever since I met you." He ran his mouth down the middle of her chest, leaving a trail of kisses over her hip bones then peeled her panties off. She bucked again as his mouth enveloped her and he brought her to climax within minutes. Once she crashed into her orgasm, calling his name he followed it with another slower exploration of her long, lean body, giving her as much pleasure as she could stand

and then some. Eventually, he couldn't deny himself any longer and when she guided him into her heat the truth of the moment wasn't lost on him. They both moved slowly, savoring each wave of pleasure before they fell together into the emotions and sensations that had been building for months. He belonged to her. She owned him.

Chapter Eighteen

C HARLOTTE WOKE UP to the sound of her phone alarm chiming; she vaguely remembered hitting the snooze button once or twice. Looking around, her eyes searched her quiet bedroom for Caleb, even though she knew she was alone in her apartment. He woke the first time her alarm went off and after the hottest morning sex she could ever remember having, he left to go home and change before work.

Making her way to her bathroom, her limbs felt heavy and her muscles ached as if she'd overexerted herself the day before. Her body wasn't used to being flexed in the masterful ways Caleb made love, but that didn't discourage her from wanting more. The memory of his mouth and hands all over her and the pleasure he evoked, forced a smile on her lips.

Looking at the clock again, she resigned to be late but forced herself to do the bare minimum so she was out the door within thirty minutes. After a quick shower, and her hair in a stylish fussy bun, she opted to apply makeup on the train. Even after she raced to get to the station two blocks from her building, she almost missed her stop as she replayed all the ways Caleb touched her. She bypassed her favorite coffee shop and vowed to deal with the office brew for the day because she didn't want to be any later than she already was.

Her phone dinged with a text just as she arrived in her office and Caleb's name flashed across the screen, but her colleague Nina was waiting for her at her desk.

"What's wrong?" Charlotte said, feeling the glow from the night before slipping away.

"The Italians are disrupting the Amalfi project timeline because they're unhappy with the language we chose for the campaign," Nina said with a grimace.

"One of our biggest projects in Europe was complete as of Friday and now the Italians decide they're too prudish for our sexy slogan? Is this opposite day?" Charlotte asked.

"Apparently our slogan is a bit sacrilegious. They have requested we rethink it," Nina said.

"How much will that cost us?"

Charlotte looked down at her phone and opened the text from Caleb.

"Please meet me for a coffee this morning."

"Did you hear me? It will cost us 100,000 Euro to change the slogan now," Nina cringed.

"Well, we're not doing that." Normally she wouldn't run off to see the man she just slept with during work—not an everyday occurrence for her, but since he spoke fluent Italian and understood the culture, she decided it was necessary.

"We need to brainstorm as many ideas as possible. Maybe we could potentially add to the already existing slogan, like another word in a different color."

Nina nodded before sitting at her desk to start drafting options.

Charlotte set her bag down and texted Caleb back. "Can you meet me in an hour? I'm having a small crisis and could use your Italian language skills."

"Anytime, anywhere, *bella*," Caleb replied.

Charlotte's heart skipped and a warmth of emotion spread through her body. The man was hot enough to make her melt via text.

An hour later Charlotte walked out to the coffee stand across the street from the Cavalier building. Caleb stood holding two coffee cups, and wearing a sexy familiar smile. The cold air hit her heated neck as she recalled his mouth on her most private lady parts from the night before.

Women passing by did double-takes to look at him and several paused to admire the gorgeousness of a well-dressed attractive man in an impeccable suit and plush winter overcoat. His eyes sparkled in the late-morning sun. She itched to pull his scarf to bring his mouth closer to hers but resisted.

"Good morning," he said, his voice deeper than usual and she wondered if he was thinking about how he had her trembling with desire the night before.

"You're in a good mood," she said.

"I'm happy you agreed to meet me, even if it's only for my Italian skills," Caleb teased.

She laughed and accepted the coffee he held out to her. A jolt from the slight touch of his hand sent a shiver through her body. He moved closer, putting his arm on the small of her back to guide her down a path carved into a park.

"Do you have time to sit with me?" Caleb asked.

"Yes, but I really do need your help with something."

"I'm all yours," Caleb said.

The innuendo was clear. Charlotte wanted to kiss his smug lips but didn't dare risk someone from the office catching them.

"Privileges of being a VP, no fires to put out this morning?" she asked.

He arched one sexy eyebrow at her. "How can I help?"

They sat on a concrete bench set under a large maple tree in the middle of the small park. His coat was unbuttoned and he casually blew on his hot coffee. All she could think about was kissing his pursed lips and tucking herself into his warmth.

Trying not to stare or get too distracted, she opened the striped leather case holding her digital tablet where she had several slogans written out.

"This project is under scrutiny at the eleventh hour because one of the Italian counterparts decided our slogan is too sexy. We attempted to google the Italian translation for all of these, but I wanted your opinion before we go back to the Italians."

Caleb accepted the tablet and read the slogans. He made a few small edits on the translations and then read them aloud.

"Faith in our decadence and your pleasure.

"Fede nella nostra decadenza e nel tuo piacere."

"This is the current slogan, and everything was approved. Now someone on their end is kowtowing to one prudish opinion and it will cost Cavalier a small fortune to completely scrap it." She explained.

"What's your plan?" His eyes studied her, and she enjoyed his confidence in her.

"If we make an addition to the slogan, the signs won't need to all be remade and rehung. Even the linens, menus, and napkins can have a word added, instead of creating all new."

"Very smart. Let's see our options. I assume they're upset with the use of the word faith, a bit of a stretch but we don't want to delay the project's completion over a slogan. As we learned years ago, the Italians can really drag their feet on permits and approvals if they want to," he said, referencing the project they worked on together in Rome when they first met.

"Right. So we thought up the following additions. What do you think?"

He read over the top two options she included on the main page. He didn't need to know they had brainstormed another ten options.

Faith in our decadence and your pleasure... In love.

Faith in our decadence and your pleasure... Loving life.

"Are they too corny?"

"No, they're smart and thoughtful. Italian culture can be, by American standards, indulgent in all aspects of life. Love is cherished and celebrated just as much as pleasure is. Sometimes those two concepts are at odds."

Caleb jotted down a few words: Cherished. Pleasure. Indulgence.

"I like cherished. It implies more of a tender commitment," Charlotte said, leaning closer to him to see what he wrote.

"I agree. What about this?"

Faith in our decadence and your pleasure… Cherishing you.

Fede nella nostra decadenza e nel vostoro piacere… Amarti.

Listening to him translate the Italian was like pouring lighter fluid on a fire. She was captivated by his mouth and what she already knew it was capable of.

"I love it," Charlotte said, clearing her throat.

She watched as he finished writing the slogan in Italian for her.

"There is only one problem," she said.

"What?" Caleb met her gaze.

"You're better at this than me."

"No, I just added to your genius." He moved his hand onto her leg, warming her skin beneath her fitted suit pants.

"Unfortunately, I'll have to give you credit for this one, but we can blame it on your intimate knowledge of Italian."

"Maybe we should go to Amalfi to convince the prude that our slogan has no intention of offending even the most pious Italian," Caleb said.

"Not a terrible idea, but I doubt either of us could take that much time away from work."

"Let's see how they react to your plan, but if an in-person meeting is necessary, I will fall on that sword with you." His eyes dazzled with mischief and his lips spread wide.

"I think I'll provide the Italians two options to choose from."

"That's a good plan. Let them see you worked on offering them an alternative," Caleb said.

"Thank you."

"I want to kiss you," he said as they stared into each other's eyes.

"I want you to kiss me, but I don't want to risk someone from the office seeing us," she said, sipping her coffee to distract herself.

"You want to keep a low profile for now?" Caleb asked.

"I think it's for the best. I know it wouldn't impact how people treat you but I think it's bad optics if my colleagues see me making out with a VP. They'll judge all my work against what favoritism they think I could gain from being attached to you."

"I understand, but it doesn't mean I like it. I do like the part where you are attached to me."

She laughed.

"Can I see you tomorrow night for dinner? We can start kissing before I cook for you."

"I look forward to it." Charlotte stood. "I better go before I change my mind about my reputation."

Caleb stood and handed her the tablet, then picked up her coffee and handed it to her.

"I am responsible enough to make sure we don't tarnish your reputation until you're ready." He closed the space between them but didn't touch her. "Because at some point we'll need to acknowledge our relationship publicly." his eyes were intense, and he studied her reaction.

She craned her neck to look up and forced a grin. "Are you coming back to the office?"

"No, you go ahead. I'm going to run an errand before I head back," he said.

"Okay, see you tomorrow. Thank you for the coffee and your help."

"Thank you for joining me."

She could feel his eyes on her as she made her way across the street, but she didn't look back. A knot developed in her stomach the instant he mentioned a relationship. Sleeping together meant more than just a hookup to both of them, but hearing him say it, only solidified that she was moving beyond Sam. Half of her was giddy at the idea of being with Caleb and belonging to him, but the other half was terrified. She couldn't talk to her colleagues and didn't feel comfortable calling one of her old friends, most of whom were married to cops or she'd lost touch with after Sam died. Sadly, her main confidant was Marco or her brother Conner—but that would have to wait until after she dealt with the Italians.

Chapter Nineteen

O N WEDNESDAY AFTER work, Charlotte made her way to Caleb's apartment via train. He lived in a posh neighborhood, and she was eager to be surrounded by his things. All day at work her mind flitted to thoughts of him, and she wondered if there was anything about him that would bother her. Like, what if he was a neat freak or worse the total opposite? What if he had a weird collection of coffee mugs or what if he was even more stylish and sexy than she thought, what if she didn't fit into his life? These were the thoughts that plagued her ever since he mentioned they were in a relationship.

"I'm glad you're here," Caleb said after meeting her in the lobby of his building. "I know there are a million amazing restaurants in this city but I thought it'd be nice to cook for you."

"And he cooks," Charlotte said with awe, following him through the swanky all-white marble and glass lobby, manned by a concierge, into a waiting elevator.

"I can change a flat tire too if that increases my ranking in your mind," Caleb said.

"Very impressive. I'm looking forward to seeing where you live. I need to confirm you're not crazy before this goes any further."

His warm hand enveloped hers as they rode up the elevator. She wondered if the nervous charge of energy coursing through her would simmer down any time soon. Her entire body responded when she was around him, and now nothing was standing in their way.

"You're falling right into my trap," he teased.

"I like a man with a plan."

"I've got lots of plans, baby." His use of the playful nickname sent shivers through her.

Although he probably didn't expect it, she had a master plan of her own once they got up to his place and nothing was going to deter her.

Following him through the door the impressive gourmet style kitchen was to her right and the foyer led into a large living room with high ceilings, a wall of windows, a plush rug, and a large comfortable-looking couch. After helping her with her coat, he hung it by the door while she took in her surroundings. His place was much bigger than hers, with a modern kitchen, floating gas stove on an island that looked out into a large living room, and honey-brown wood floors. There was a patio with two curved chairs looking out into the city where the sky colored everything in pink and orange light from the last remnants of the sun.

"Make yourself at home. I was just getting started on our dinner." Soft acoustic music played on the hidden speakers. She walked farther into the living room to look at the hundreds of books he had stacked on the built-in shelves. There was a family picture prominently displayed in front of his collection of novels, some with Italian titles.

"Did you read all of these?" she asked, holding the picture of his family.

"Most of them. Some were gifts from my grandmother; she loved to read. As a kid she would take me to the library every weekend and always insisted that you could go anywhere with a good book."

Setting the picture back down, she moved over to the kitchen to be close to him. He poured them each a glass of wine, and she watched as he chopped things then tossed dozens of ingredients into a large pot. Soon the entire apartment smelled of garlic, curry, and scents she didn't recognize.

"Are you making me Indian food?" Charlotte asked.

"Yes, is that okay? I had this amazing biryani chicken on a trip to London once, and I learned how to make it during my many lonely years in Rome."

"Oh, poor gorgeous Caleb, alone in the city of Roman ruins surrounded by beautiful Italian women." She walked into his arms and kissed his chin.

"Surrounded by beautiful women, yes, but the one woman I needed wasn't there," he said, kissing each of her eyes, then her cheeks before his mouth landed on her lips.

"Your romantic side is dangerous, and these sexy eyes with your long lashes are lethal. A girl could lose herself and her panties all at once."

Caleb stretched to turn the pot down to simmer. "Now that you mention it." He slid his other hand down the back side of her jeans and pulled her in closer. His mouth possessed hers in a kiss that felt consuming.

Before she could comment, he hoisted her up over his

shoulder and smacked her bottom.

"Let me give you the full tour." He stalked out of the kitchen to what she assumed was the bedroom and she didn't mind.

✕

THE NEXT MORNING Charlotte woke in Caleb's bed to the sound of him making coffee. The sun was rising and streams of morning light began to peek through the long curtains in his otherwise dark room. After using the bathroom, she gathered her discarded clothes, pulled on her jeans from the night before, and he appeared with a cup of coffee.

"You're a morning person?" she asked.

He was already dressed in another impeccable suit with a light salmon tie that set off his gorgeous skin tone, and she made a point to try not to drool.

Caleb laughed. "Does that surprise you?" he asked, handing her the steaming cup but kissed her before letting it go. "Good morning."

"Good morning. They do say waking up early is a trait of most successful people."

"What else do they say?" he asked, moving closer and kissing her neck.

She sipped the hot brew. "That I'll be late if I don't scoot out of here to get home and get ready. I didn't plan on sleeping over, sorry."

"It was late, you were tired, and don't be sorry."

"As I recall, you coaxed me into a sedated stupor with your mouth," she said.

Caleb smiled. "I'll come to your place next so it's fair." He winked.

Charlotte felt the awkwardness of the moment settle over them.

When would be the next time, were they officially dating, would they spend more and more nights together? Did she want that?

"Okay," was all she came up with. She set her coffee in the kitchen and grabbed her purse before slipping on her shoes.

"Hang on, I'll walk you down." In the kitchen, Caleb grabbed an insulated travel mug and poured her coffee into it, and then pocketed his keys. Next, he grabbed his own coat and held the door for her.

In the elevator, he smiled and moved closer to her as an older woman joined them on the fourth floor with her fluffy white dog on a pink leash.

"Good morning," the woman said. Her polished look screamed New York, while Charlotte was still wearing one of Caleb's T-shirts under her coat and sporting bedhead.

"Good morning," Caleb replied politely while slipping an arm around Charlotte.

He had another greeting for the concierge and held her hand while they walked out to the cold but busy street. Lastly, he pulled her in for a long kiss, and she forgot for a moment it was a weekday morning. She tasted mint and coffee on his full, firm mouth and enjoyed the feel of his protective arm around her back before she remembered she was due to be at work in an hour.

"Dinner, tonight? Your place?" Caleb asked, still kissing

her lips.

"Sure." She didn't know what else to say. She knew she wanted to be with him; even the idea of waiting ten hours so they could both go to work sounded terrible.

"Good I want to maximize our time together before you head home for Christmas next week and my family converges on me." Caleb's satisfied smile dazzled her before he turned to hail a cab and she watched dumbfounded. He was so attentive and delicious.

"Have a great morning." He handed her the travel mug and gave her another kiss before opening the taxi door. Once he closed her door, he reached into the front seat to tell the driver where her apartment was and handed him money.

"Bye," was all she could think to say and buckled her seat belt.

Caleb stood on the sidewalk and watched her taxi pull away.

"I could get used to this," Charlotte said to herself.

CALEB MOVED THROUGH his day in a funk. Something was off. He and Charlotte were spending almost every night together. They were getting to really know each other, and it seemed like she had let her past go. She was silly with him and open about her desire for him, which didn't explain why he was plagued with dread. He couldn't put his finger on it, but he had the distinct feeling something bad was going to happen.

"Sir, did you want to see the rubies?" the woman behind

the jewelry counter asked with a knowing smile. She must have pegged him for an easy sale when he walked in and said he needed a gift.

"Cal, are you sure you want to buy such an expensive gift after dating less than a month? I mean I know you've been obsessed with Charlotte for years but still."

The saleswoman narrowed her eyes at Marco and tsked as she brought out a tray of sparkling red ruby earrings.

"Yes, I'm sure. An expensive piece of jewelry is a symbol of a man's interest; it's sentimental and timeless. Not to mention the easiest thing to buy." He knew the last bit would make sense to Marco but in truth he wanted to spoil Charlotte. He wanted to buy her anything she wanted and lavish her with tokens of his devotion. Jewelry seemed perfect.

"Then choose something, because we still have several more stops," Marco groaned before stalking off.

Looking down at the tray, he was drawn to a simple pair of stud earrings in the shape of tears; the red was bright, and the yellow gold reminded him of Christmas time. "These are perfect," he said.

The saleswoman's smile indicated she was pleased with his selection. He wasn't sure if that was due to the price or style.

"Excellent taste. I'll remove the tag and get this wrapped for you, then ring you up."

He nodded and felt his phone vibrate as he moved down away from the counter. It was a text from Charlotte. He left work early to get her a gift since she wouldn't be staying in the city for Christmas.

Will I see you tonight? she asked.

I'll pick up dinner on my way over after this meeting. He didn't tell her he was shopping for her gift.

No, just come straight over. I don't want to wait any longer than I have to, she replied.

He couldn't help but chuckle. They were unable to get enough of each other.

"Cal, pay the woman so we can move along," Marco said, interrupting his thoughts of Charlotte waiting for him naked in bed.

"Sorry, Marco. I'm going to have to ditch you after this."

"Dude, you only got one person a gift. Can't you two spend one night apart so we can finish all this shopping?"

"Apparently not." Caleb handed over his card as the woman rang him up. He accepted the small gift bag and slipped it into his coat. "You were only going to shop for yourself anyway. You can do that faster without me holding you back."

"True. Tell Charlotte I said hello," Marco said before walking away.

He was in a taxi moments later and on his way to Charlotte's.

Get undressed. I'm on my way, he texted her.

She sent back a picture of her ceiling. *This is my view. I'm two steps ahead of you. I'll have to think of something to do while I wait,* she texted.

The mental picture of her lying in bed and touching herself while she waited for him was enough to make him groan.

You will pay for teasing me, he replied.

Mmm, I can't wait.

An hour later they lay covered in a sheen of sweat, their limbs tangled together. He smiled at the look of pure contentment on her face as she lay half on top of him.

"I lied to you," he whispered, and her eyes popped open. "I wasn't at a meeting earlier. I was getting your Christmas present, but I don't want to wait to give it to you."

"Oh." He watched as her concern was replaced by curiosity.

"I forgive you," she said.

Her playfulness was an aspect of her personality that he had forgotten about since their time in Rome. Unraveling from her body he walked naked to where he'd discarded his coat in the living room and retrieved the gift. Hiding the bag behind him as he walked back in toward her, she pulled the sheet up and watched him intently.

"This might be the best Christmas gift presentation I've ever had," she said, her hand sliding up the coiled muscle of his thigh.

He handed her the gift before pulling back the sheet and moving to lay between her thighs. Balancing above her, he looked down where she held the gift bag on her chest.

"Open it," he said, nudging her with his body.

Her eyes glossed over with lust, and she quickly plucked out the black tissue paper, retrieved the small gold box, and tossed the bag aside. Looking into her eyes, he pushed closer then stilled. Her mouth fell open and she let out a little gasp before rocking her hips up to meet him.

"First open it," he said, his voice husky with need.

She opened the box and her eyes grew wide. "Caleb, these are stunning but it's too much."

"No, they're just enough, for now." He pushed inside her and gulped at the force of emotion that pulsed through him.

They didn't speak again but instead, let their passion drive them into ecstasy. He couldn't tell her yet but he planned to spoil her every day for the rest of her life.

Chapter Twenty

LEADING UP TO Christmas, the work days grew long as everyone prepared for the holiday break, and her nights were even longer with Caleb. He managed to make it seem routine for them to take turns staying at each other's places, and by the time she even thought to leave, she was too satiated from their epic sex and exhausted to bother. Being with Caleb was completely different than being with Sam. Maybe it was because she'd grown up with Sam and they learned about what it meant to make love and enjoy sex together. Or maybe it was because she'd had a dry spell for two years as a widow, but sex with Caleb was all-consuming, hungry, can't get enough of each other kind of sex. Caleb had a confidence about him that instantly put her at ease and a tendency to entice her to want to savor every intimate moment.

On Friday she was determined to have a night to herself, if for no other reason than to make sure she could still spend time alone. She craved Caleb more each day. At work, she would watch the clock counting down to when she would get to see him. Once they were alone, they were unable to keep their hands off each other. He was a giving lover, and she was uninhibited by his attention; he made her want more. Years after losing Sam and the solitary life she created, she no longer worried about trying not to feel. She wanted to feel everything with Caleb. But she also worried that getting consumed by a new relationship could be dangerous for her independence. That afternoon Renee and Nina invited her to join them for drinks, and it was the perfect way to create some space while getting to know them better.

The more things progressed with Caleb the more she missed having girlfriends to talk to about their romance. She lost most of her friends after Sam died. Many of them were married to other cops or from her hometown and the subject of Sam always came up. At some point, she got sick of always being treated like a sad widow and pushed people away while throwing herself into her work. Maybe some of them also didn't like the reminder that their husbands had such dangerous jobs and let the friendships fade. Either way, she'd lost Sam by force, then lost friends by choice and circumstance. Moving to New York was the final step in severing ties to her old life, but that didn't mean she shouldn't seek out new friendships. She had established a nice working rapport with the PR team over the years but knew friendships would be better for a long, trusting work relationship. She could use a few girlfriends living in a big city. She couldn't let her world become just about Caleb no matter how tempting he was.

"We'll see you at the bar soon, right?" Nina asked, leaning into the doorway of Charlotte's office with her coat on and purse over her shoulder.

"Yes, I'm just finishing this last email and I'll be there," Charlotte said.

"Renee is getting a table, so don't take too long."

Charlotte looked up. "Renee is already there?"

Nina laughed. "Yeah. It's Friday, and even workaholics take a break on Fridays after six."

Charlotte grabbed her bag. "In that case, let's go."

Nina laughed. "Atta girl."

There was no point in finishing her email to Renee now, if her boss was already off the clock.

They chatted about the workweek on the short walk to a local bar which Nina said a lot of Cavalier colleagues frequented. Charlotte checked her phone as they arrived and realized she missed a text from Caleb.

How was your day?

She tucked her phone away as Nina led her through the bar to a high-top table and decided she would fire off a response once she was settled with a drink.

"I'm so glad you joined us. This is where we really get to know each other," Renee said as a waiter brought a tray of drinks. "What is your drink of choice for a Friday night out?"

Charlotte settled into her seat. "Dirty martini, please."

The waiter winked. "Coming right up."

"Stiff choice," Renee said, setting a glass of red wine in front of Nina and sipping a blue drink in a rocks glass.

"Do you two come here every Friday, and did I just rate the invite?" Charlotte asked.

"Maybe," they both said, taking sips of their drinks and looking guilty.

The bartender reappeared with her martini, and they all gave a cheers to the weekend. Renee shared her war stories of fighting her way up the ranks over the years and told a funny story about her first boss when she arrived at Cavalier a decade before. Although they were each at different phases of their career, and Renee was clearly in charge, tonight it felt like three women with shared interests taking a break. Charlotte sipped her drink wondering if she could risk texting Caleb back while sitting at a cramped table with two of their colleagues. Seconds later her phone began to ring in her bag, and she knew exactly who it would be but felt bad ignoring it.

"Go on, take the call. We'll pretend not to listen," Renee teased. Just then another woman's boisterous squeal at the bar distracted them.

Charlotte plucked her phone out of her bag. "Hi, I'm sorry I didn't respond earlier. I just got caught up at work and a few colleagues invited me for drinks.

"No problem, I'm still at the office," Caleb said.

"You must be exhausted. It's been a long week," she said.

"It has. I forgot to mention my sister is coming to town tomorrow. Can you have dinner with us?" He asked, followed by a "please."

Granted he had already met her entire family at her brother's Friendsgiving, but it seemed like a big step to meet his sister. She had the impression he was very close with his only sibling, but she couldn't think of a good excuse to say no.

"I don't want to be a third wheel. I'm sure your sister would rather have you all to herself."

"She specifically said she wanted to meet you, but don't worry she's not on a SWAT team or a Navy SEAL."

She laughed before agreeing and noticed Renee and Nina were making cheesy faces at her and listening to every word.

"Alright, have fun out with the girls. I'm heading home now if you want to come by after," Caleb said.

He sounded casually optimistic, and she felt a tingle of expectation at the idea of meeting him in bed.

"We'll see how late it is," she said.

"Okay, have fun."

She hung up before she could feel bad about being guarded on the phone.

"Tell us about this mystery man that wants you to meet his sister," Renee said.

"You work fast. One month in New York and you already have a man after your Friday nights and introducing you to the family. Maybe you can give your two new best friends some tips," Nina teased.

Charlotte's cheeks heated with embarrassment. "It's new." Charlotte went to sip her drink and realized it was gone.

"New and hot I bet, especially if he's introducing you to the family," Nina said.

Charlotte eyed their server and held up her glass. He winked and nodded. She was walking a tightrope by seeing Caleb and talking about it with her colleagues, but she knew Nina was right. Her relationship with Caleb felt serious from the start.

"You don't have to tell us, for now." Renee held up her glass to toast them just as Charlotte's second martini arrived. "But at some point, I'm going to need to hear all the juicy, sexy details because I'm having a dry spell." They all laughed before they ended up talking about all the worst dates they'd each been on and how hard it is to meet someone.

Two hours later Charlotte said good night and hopped in a taxi home, but she rattled off Caleb's address instead of her own. Even though she didn't finish the second martini, it was clear from nausea rising in her throat that one had done its damage. In college, she learned she could never just pass out like all her friends after drinking a bit too much. No matter how late it was, she would be up for hours and likely get sick. Her brothers always said she was too much of a control freak to get drunk.

"Hello, I'm going up to see, Mr. Kincaid," Charlotte said to the concierge once she arrived at Caleb's building. The polite doorman clearly couldn't care less as he buzzed her into the entrance with a wave.

Once on the seventh floor, she realized her plan to sneak into Caleb's bed was flawed because she didn't have a key. She stood outside his door and thought about the implication of spending another night with him. It probably wasn't the best idea, and then she checked the time. Eleven o'clock was a reasonable hour; she could suggest they order a pizza and cuddle. Pizza sounded amazing, so she knocked.

A minute later Caleb's groggy eyes met hers as he opened the door to reveal he was only wearing pajama pants.

Chapter Twenty-One

"HI, DO YOU want pizza?" she asked, walking inside his apartment.

Caleb laughed. "I thought I might see you tonight." He moved to the kitchen and retrieved a glass, then filled it to the top with water.

"Oh no, I've become predictable? I'll have to fix that."

"Drink this," he said, holding out the glass and she obeyed.

"Did you eat?" he asked.

"Some fries we shared at the bar."

Caleb nodded and retrieved a loaf of bread and peanut butter. He went about the task of spreading the peanut butter on one side, then a red jam from his fridge on the other side before putting each half together and cutting it down the middle from corner to corner.

"Triangles, huh. Interesting way to cut your PB&J."

He placed the sandwich in front of her at the counter.

"Eat," he said.

"Can I ask you something?"

"Anything."

"Are we officially dating, and do people still say boyfriend and girlfriend? It sounds sort of juvenile."

"Yes, we are in a serious monogamous relationship. I agree the term girlfriend does sound childish, but I would feel more awkward calling you my lover when I introduce you to my family."

She laughed and warmth flooded her at the thought of belonging to him.

"Lover," she tested the word, before taking a big bite of the sandwich he made her. "Uhhhh what is it about a PB&J that is so satisfying."

"Keep eating," he said, standing with no shirt on in the kitchen looking edible himself.

"You're very bossy tonight."

"You're drunk."

"Tipsy, not drunk. I don't like to lose control."

"I can see that. Do you feel in control now?" He leaned on the counter and watched as she sipped her water and took another big bite of the sandwich.

"Yes, I am in complete control. Do you want a bite?" She offered him her half-eaten sandwich.

"No, thank you. I'm holding out for something sweeter."

Charlotte thought about that for a moment. "Do you mean like dessert? Do you have cake here?" She looked around the tidy modern kitchen.

A sexy smirk slowly spread across his face "No cake. Do you want me to get you cake?"

"You would do that?"

"Yes," he said, standing straight up again and moving closer to her like a lion prowling.

"Because you're so nice?"

"Because you're my girlfriend and I want you to be happy. If the cake will make you happy, I'll go get it."

"You're a keeper, obviously I mean look at you." Charlotte waved her hand up and down in front of him, to emphasize his physical attributes.

He was within arm's reach, leaning against the counter and his six-pack flinched with his laughter.

"So I'll go get you cake. Anything else, princess?" he asked.

"No, this is fine. Hmm princess, I like baby better," she said.

"Okay, baby." Caleb crossed his arms over his chest and waited.

She finished her sandwich and swiped her hands together to knock off any crumbs.

"So if there is no cake, what are you having for dessert?" She looked around the kitchen and sipped her water.

Walking around the counter he took her hand and guided her to stand up.

"What do you think?" He gently tugged her hand, leading her back to his bedroom. He set her water on the bedside table and stood before her.

"I'm glad you came over. Next time text me and I'll come get you."

Caleb moved both his hands to frame her face as he placed kisses along her jawbone and then down her throat.

"I'm a big girl, I can manage," she said, closing her eyes while enjoying the sensations of his touch until she wobbled and opened her eyes again.

Gripping her arms to steady her as she swayed, concern filled his eyes. "Do you want to try to sleep?"

"No, I'll get dizzy if I lie down."

Nodding, he untucked her blouse and unfastened each button before sliding it off and setting it on the chair in the corner of his room. Next, he unzipped her skirt and slid it down her legs to the floor. Kneeling in front of her, his hands skimmed up her thighs covered by tights before pulling those down to her ankles, and helping her step out of them. The cool air hit her skin but was soon replaced by the heat of his mouth. He kneeled in front of her, placing delicate but hot kisses along her hips and over her abdomen before he spun her slowly and kissed up along her back. He brushed her hair over one shoulder while kissing her neck from behind. The sensations of his hands gripping her from behind, the scruff of his chin rubbed along her skin, and his ripped muscles pressed against her.

"Best idea ever," she said as he led her to stand with her hands against the dresser. In the dim light of the room she could barely see his reflection in the mirror but felt everything. He coaxed her body with every touch, giving her pleasure with his worship of her body.

The next morning Charlotte woke to sunlight streaming through one crack in the curtains that fell on her face. The soft sound of Caleb's steady breath next to her had her searching her brain for how she ended up in his bed. PB&J and Caleb's mouth wasn't a bad way to end a night after one too many martinis. She didn't feel hungover at all. Sliding out of bed, she made her way into the kitchen. After making a pot of coffee, she surveyed his fridge for breakfast items. Once she had the bacon cooked, she started to whip the eggs and heard Caleb stirring.

"Baby, are you wearing my T-shirt with no panties while making breakfast, or is this a dream?" Caleb asked.

He slinked into the kitchen with his dark hair mussed up and only low-slung pajama pants on. His eyes squinted from the light shining in through the floor-to-ceiling windows that looked out over the city.

"Yes, I call it bare-bottom bacon breakfast, with scrambled eggs and coffee. It's the Charlotte special."

Caleb grinned before he reached for her and pulled her against his chest in a big squeeze.

"Good morning." He kissed her neck. "Are you still drunk or are you turning into a morning person too?" he teased.

"I wasn't drunk, just a little tipsy, but I must have worked it all out with our late-night activity. I feel fine."

"You mean we sexed off your buzz?" Caleb laughed.

"I think so." She leaned up to kiss his chin before flipping the scrambled eggs over again.

"I could get used to this. I'd even be happy to make you breakfast as long as you keep walking around like this."

He reached down to lift the bottom of her T-shirt and kissed her left cheek.

"Mmmmm, good morning indeed," he said.

Turning off the stove, she felt the stirring of desire as soon as he pressed his chest against her back. She tried to pour him a cup of coffee, but he set the empty cup aside next to the stove. Looking back into his eyes they were heavy with desire. It was clear he was thinking the same thing she was when he lifted her on the counter. The granite was cool on her bare bottom, but heat pooled between her legs. He spread her thighs enough to accommodate his hips that were at just the right level. He smiled, cupping her breast through the T-shirt she wore causing her to gasp.

"Hmmm, breakfast can wait," she said.

He lifted the T-shirt over her head and pushed her back to lie down then pulled her hips against him harder. His hands roamed her body, teasing her while his mouth trailed over her throat.

"Do you hear that buzzing sound?" Charlotte said as she tried to catch her breath.

Cupping both her breasts, Caleb's chest heaved.

"It's the concierge," he said.

"He can't hear us, can he?" She cringed, lying sprawled on the island counter.

"No, thankfully," he said and kissed her hip. The buzzing continued and he groaned. "Don't move," he ordered and walked naked into the foyer. He hit a button before speaking into a small panel she never noticed.

"Yes?"

"Sir, we tried your cell first. You have company. Your sister, I believe," a nervous voice said.

"Oh shit." Caleb looked back at Charlotte, still naked on the counter.

"Your sister is here? Now?" she squeaked.

"Yes, I forgot. You distracted me with your bottom for breakfast." He laughed before telling the concierge to send his sister up.

Charlotte jumped down from the counter and gathered up their discarded clothes before handing him his pants.

"Does it smell like sex in here?" she asked.

"Nah, it smells like bacon." Caleb laughed and began getting dressed.

Charlotte ran to his room naked as he laughed louder.

"I'm getting in the shower. Wipe down the counter," she yelled.

Chapter Twenty-Two

LIKE A TORNADO, Katie rolled into his apartment with her huge suitcase and dumped everything at the front door, then promptly began grilling Caleb about the woman's shoes discarded there.

"Those are Charlotte's and we've been seeing each other for a few weeks," Caleb said, pouring himself a cup of coffee.

"You two are sleeping together, which means it's serious," Katie said, squinting at him. "I can't believe I'm just hearing about this."

"I know you're curious, but can you be a little less you and not scare her off."

"I'm just asking since last I heard you were still obsessing over her and whining about her not giving you the time of day," Katie said as the bedroom door opened and Charlotte stepped out in her wrinkled clothes from the day before.

The telltale blush on her face indicated she had at least heard the last thing his sister said if not everything.

"Charlotte, I am ecstatic to see you again." Katie walked over to where Charlotte hovered in the living room and gave her a big hug. "We have a busy day planned. We need to go Christmas shopping for our parents, get a tree, and maybe find a few fancy New Year's Eve dresses," Katie said, pointing at Charlotte.

"New Year's Eve dresses?"

"Yes, I scored tickets to a swanky party here in New York. I'm flying back to Seattle to be with my boyfriend but there is no reason you two shouldn't enjoy a night on the town," Katie beamed.

Charlotte looked at him and all he could do was shrug, having no idea what Katie was talking about.

"Why don't you tell us about this party, and we'll decide if we want to attend." Caleb carried his coffee into the living room and grabbed Charlotte's hand on his way to the couch. Setting his coffee down he sat and pulled her to sit on his lap as he wrapped his arms around her.

Meanwhile, Katie dug through her bag for something.

"You think I'm bossy," he said, burying his face in her neck, "wait until you spend a day with my little sister. She makes Genghis Khan look like a baby doll," Caleb said. Charlotte was stiff with nervous energy which he found endearing, but he didn't want her to be uncomfortable around his family.

"I heard that," Katie called from the kitchen where she grabbed a plate. "I'm just going to help myself to some of this breakfast if you two aren't going to eat it."

"Go ahead," Caleb said as Charlotte elbowed him. He started laughing and slid his hands up her arms, kissing along her bare neck. "I like your hair up like this; it gives me better access." He felt her body shiver in response and wished his sister would go take a nap.

"Caleb, your sister is trying to eat." She turned her head to chastise him, creating easier access for him to capture her mouth with his. Her body responded, and she kissed him back with matching desire.

"Okay, love birds, here are your tickets." Katie dropped two black envelopes on Charlotte's lap and sat next to them. Her plate was piled high with toast, eggs, and bacon.

"That looks good," Caleb said teasingly.

"I know right." Katie gestured to Charlotte. "She's a keeper." Picking up her toast smeared with butter, she took a huge bite.

Caleb watched as Charlotte opened one of the envelopes and pulled out a black and white invitation embossed with gold lettering. There was an address with an odd barcode at the bottom, and that was it.

"Cool invite, right?" Katie said.

"Whose party is this?" Caleb asked.

Katie's eyes grew big with excitement. "You remember my roommate in college? Well, she has done very well for herself in creating this exclusive party scene that specializes in over-the-top VIP parties for the rich and famous. My boyfriend has to work on Christmas, but he said he would make it up to me on New Year's Eve, so I can't stay. I'm gifting you both my tickets," Katie said dramatically like she had bestowed a royal title on them.

Charlotte inspected the invitation with an approving eye. "I've never been to a big party for New Year's Eve."

"It will be so epic." Katie's enthusiasm was competing with her appetite as she devoured the rest of her breakfast.

"Will you be back in town in time for New Year's?" Caleb asked Charlotte. "If not, I could catch the train and meet you in Virginia."

"There is no way I can spend an entire week at home living with my parents again," Charlotte laughed.

"Great, then you can both go." Katie gulped Caleb's coffee, satisfied with her meal. "Now, can we please do some shopping?"

"Fine, but we don't need a tree," Caleb said.

When Katie and Charlotte frowned at him with similar expressions, he almost enjoyed the idea of being wrong.

"Of course we need a tree. Do you want Mom to cry for Christmas? What did those Italians do to your holiday spirit?" Katie said.

Charlotte sat, laughing on his lap and he liked that she relaxed quickly. Maybe his sister's over-the-top personality was good for something.

"I agree if you're hosting your family for Christmas, you need some more decorations." Charlotte stood and smoothed her rumpled blouse. "I would love to tag along but I need to go home and change. Maybe I can meet up with you two later."

"Maybe? Charlotte, I need your help shopping for a dress!" Katie said.

"And I need your help distracting her or my apartment will look like the North Pole," Caleb said, tugging on her hand.

He could see her uncertainty and he wanted to reassure her it would be fun, but he didn't want to pressure her into something she didn't want to do.

"Okay, if you're sure I'm not interfering in your sibling time," she said, looking to Katie for confirmation.

"Oh no, we'll have the entire week to get on each other's

nerves." Katie smiled and carried her plate to the kitchen.

"You're sure I'm not going to be in the way?" Charlotte asked for only him to hear.

"Positive." He kissed her worried lips. "Did you already buy gifts for your parents and brothers?"

"No, I think I've been too distracted to track that Christmas is only a week away." She cringed and her nose scrunched up.

Caleb stood and enveloped Charlotte in his arms with his back to his sister. "You better go now before I drag you back into my room for another distraction." He kissed her before letting go. "Meet us at Macy's when you're ready."

Charlotte looked up from his embrace. "Won't it be a madhouse there?"

"Yep, and Katie will take like two hours to decide which insanely huge Lego set to get my dad for Christmas morning. Then they'll have pieces scattered everywhere and give up by noon and I'll be forced to finish it."

"I'm sensing a family tradition," Charlotte laughed.

"Yup, maybe next year you can join us and help me." He didn't even think about the implication of what he said; it just slipped out. Charlotte's eyes grew big with surprise, but he didn't regret it. He wanted her in his life a year from now, and another five years. He was fairly certain he wanted her forever. He just needed to be careful not to scare her with anything too serious yet.

"I'm pretty good with puzzles but I don't think I've ever done an entire Lego set," she said, recovering from her initial shock.

"Interesting. If you promise to be a little naughty later,

I'll see if I can find a set for us to do," Caleb teased.

"You're going to reward me for being naughty?"

"As long as I'm the one that gets to enjoy your naughti-ness, like last night when you—" Charlotte's hand clamped over his mouth to stop him from finishing his sentence and he laughed before kissing the inside of her palm.

"I better go or we're going to traumatize your sister," Charlotte said, heading for the door.

Caleb swatted her bottom as she walked into the kitchen where Katie stood smirking while looking at her phone and sipping a fresh cup of coffee.

"See you soon," Katie called.

"Your guest room is to the right in the hallway. I'm just going to walk Charlotte out," Caleb said to his sister before helping Charlotte put her coat on and grabbing his own. In the elevator, he couldn't resist pushing her up against the wall and stealing a few kisses. She had invaded his thoughts when they weren't together, and he couldn't keep his hands off her when they were together.

"Maybe you should come back with me to my place and help me get changed," she said before nipping his ear.

"You're addictive," he whispered as the elevator doors opened and she slipped out of his arms.

"Right back at you." She pressed the number of his floor and laughed. "Bye for now baby," she called as she walked away.

✕

CHARLOTTE COULDN'T REMEMBER the last time she had so

much fun shopping, which made her sad that the last two years of her life were so empty. It made perfect sense to mourn the loss of Sam, his life, and the love they shared, but it had been at the expense of her own life.

She let her heartbreak supersede every aspect of her life. Somehow Caleb broke through her fog and got her to have fun again; she found her joy again. She wasn't the same woman that fell in love with the boy next door, but she wasn't just the sad widow anymore either.

"Baby, which tree do you like the best?" Caleb asked, breaking through her thoughts.

They were standing in a pop-up tree stand near his apartment and he was holding out his arms to point at two large trees. At some point he just accepted his apartment was going to look like Santa's workshop and started getting into the idea of picking out decorations.

He stood smiling, looking like he belonged on a Christmas card in his gray wool coat with a red Santa hat, and red scarf, surrounded by trees.

"Maybe we should ask Katie since I won't be there to enjoy it with you this year."

Closing the space between them, he looped his arms around her waist pulling her close. "Don't remind me." His warm mouth pressed several kisses on her neck before the tree lot owner coughed to interrupt them.

"We'll take that one," Charlotte said, pointing to the tree she thought was the fullest. "How are we going to get this back to your apartment?" She leaned into his arms still around her waist.

Katie walked up and handed Charlotte a hot chocolate.

"We still need decorations for the tree and there is another pop-up a block away."

Caleb sighed. "I'll carry the tree back while you two can choose the ornaments and maybe an angel for the top. Then meet me back at the apartment and we'll order dinner." He kissed Charlotte before walking away to purchase the tree and leaving her with his sister.

"Finally, we're alone," Katie said with a wicked smile. "Ask me anything you want to know."

A few hours later Charlotte and Caleb sat on his couch in the dark, staring at the colorful lights they'd strung on the tall Christmas tree set up in the corner. Katie crashed soon after dinner, and Charlotte stuck around to help him decorate the tree and clean up all the pine needles that fell in the process of dragging it into his apartment.

"Your sister is a character," she said as she snuggled farther into his chest.

He ran his hand up and down her back, and she could hear the thump of his heartbeat beneath her cheek.

"She was on her best behavior today. Wait until you really get to know her."

"When do your folks arrive?"

"Wednesday, too bad you'll miss them. I would've liked to introduce you to them on this trip. Who knows when they'll be back in town. All those years of living in the suburbs and now they're world travelers."

She could hear the smile in his voice.

"I'm dreading the train ride back to Virginia, but I think it's better than driving," Charlotte said.

Caleb pulled her up along his body so her face hovered

over his and their chests were pressed together. "We better make the most of the next four days before your trip."

He pulled her mouth down to his, and she wondered how she ever resisted him before. Raising her knees up, she straddled his hips. The twinkling lights of the tree competed with the stars she saw as Caleb drove her desire for him to overwhelming heights. They just barely made it to his room before she was completely naked and begging him for more.

Chapter Twenty-Three

F IVE DAYS BEFORE Christmas his doctor destroyed him with three horrible words. "You have cancer."

He had melanoma, the worst type of skin cancer a person can get because it's basically a tumor and can spread fast. After dropping that bomb on him, his doctor recommended surgery the same day; she had an opening in her schedule that afternoon. Although the original spot on his shoulder had been removed, the doctor wanted to remove a larger area to be sure they got everything. He agreed and spent the morning sitting in the waiting room of the medical center's surgery space, watching people coming and going, wondering why they were there and if they were dying. Worse did he look like he was dying?

Nurses prepared his shoulder for surgery, and then his doctor cut out the offensive spot with "good margins" to make sure they got it all. Lying in the cold room as the doctor stitched up his shoulder, all he could feel was the faint sensation of his skin being pulled. The entire time she explained the additional tests she would need to run to determine if the cancer had spread and to where in his body.

All the while an emptiness settled over him. He finally convinced Charlotte to date him, she let down her walls, and now this. Instead of worrying if it was too early to tell her he loved her, he worried if he would live long enough to know what it might be like to be loved by her.

The doctor's voice sounded like she was talking through a wall, and he barely heard a word she said as she bandaged up his shoulder.

"There are more tests we'll need to run."

"How long will it take to know if the cancer has spread?" he asked, sitting up when she was done.

"Mr. Kincaid, you have to take things slow right now," she cautioned him.

He pinned her with his eyes and knew he was projecting desperation, but he didn't care.

The doctor exhaled. "As I said we'll send the sample to the lab to confirm we got all the cancer from this location. The scans we took when you arrived will determine if there are any additional areas on the dermis that we also need to worry about and potentially remove. Then we need to run more tests to determine if it metastasized or spread to any other area of your body."

"Please run every test. But how long for the results?" he persisted.

She took a deep breath. "Usually it takes five to seven days. But with the Christmas holiday, it's likely we won't get results until the 28th or 29th of December."

Hanging his head, he looked down at the ground and cursed.

"But it might take until the New Year," the doctor added.

"That's almost two weeks. Is there a way to expedite

this?"

The doctor shook her head. "No, Mr. Kincaid, this isn't the kind of thing we can put a rush on. The labs are always booked solid. There is no skipping to the front of the line."

"And what is your gut feeling, your expert opinion?" he pressed her.

"I don't see any additional cancerous lesions on the surface of your skin, but I can't begin to guess if the cancer has spread." The woman spoke in a detached manner. "I will say the sample we took was judged to be at the earliest stage possible. Coupled with your age and darker skin tone, you are far less likely to have a metastasized melanoma, but there are always exceptions."

"Damn it." Standing up from the operating table, his shoulder throbbed as he grabbed his dress shirt.

"Do you know of any family history of skin cancer, or any other cancers?" the doctor asked.

"No."

"Good, that's also in your favor," she said, adding notes to her laptop.

"And if it has spread, are we talking chemo and radiation, then I die in a few years?"

"Chemo and radiation are usually reserved for late stages of cancer. Immunotherapies are recommended first before more aggressive options. I understand you have a million questions, Mr. Kincaid, and that this is difficult news but dwelling on the what-ifs will only cause you more worry. Once we have determined if the cancer has spread, we can review all the treatment options."

Nodding he fought the anger that bubbled up in his

chest. As a child the doctors found a tumor in his kidney and removed it, but at seven he'd never realized how deadly cancer could be. As an adult he knew enough to know that if the melanoma spread to places like his bones or his organs, he was a goner. Maybe the doctors could buy him a few years with treatment, but he'd be sick all the time, and in the end, cancer would get him.

"Are we done for today? Are there any other doctors I should see now? Maybe a shaman?"

The doctor handed him a card that read cancer therapist. "I recommend you see any kind of therapist or healer that will help you get through the next ten days, until we know more. I have patients that have combined Eastern medicine with our treatment plans that are still alive today. It is your health, your decision."

Looking into the young doctor's eyes, he wanted to be sure she understood his desperation. "The woman of my dreams just started giving me the time of day, so I'd hate to die and miss my life with her."

The doctor studied him. "I'll call you as soon as we have any news, no matter what day or time it is."

"Thank you," he said but the fear had already slipped in. After three weeks with Charlotte, he knew a lifetime wouldn't be enough. She was, without a doubt his person, and he had so badly wanted to be hers. He prayed she would let him into her world and hoped she would eventually need him too, but now it seemed selfish to want her.

Leaving the doctor's office, everything looked different to him. People rushed to get to work as he slowly made his way past the train station, opting to walk. Why bother racing to work, why worry about any of it if he was dying? His eyes scanned the street looking for something and landed on a pink storefront with various cakes on display. Bingo.

After walking inside, he was pleased to see the line was short. He eyed the various cakes and cookies in the display case and contemplated his options. When it was his turn, he surprised the clerk by ordering one of every cupcake and a coffee. Paying a hundred and fifty dollars for forty cupcakes seemed a bit silly when he carried the four large pink boxes to the only open table. But when he lifted the top of a box and took out a cupcake with white fluffy frosting and gold flecks, he had no regrets.

Peeling back the paper liner, he noticed the clerk stop her busy work to watch him as he took the biggest bite of the golden cake. A custard burst from the center of the cupcake, and he nodded in acknowledgment of the delicious flavors: buttercream, caramel, and vanilla. In a sad twist, the cupcake tasted how Charlotte smelled.

A twinge of regret washed over him. If his cancer had spread, he would have to give her up. It wasn't fair to expect her to sit through years of treatments only to die on her. He polished off the cupcake in two more bites and washed it down with half his coffee before exiting the shop. Hailing a taxi back to the office was his best option with four humongous cupcake boxes. He left a box with the clerks in the lobby, another two at the front desk in the executive suite where his office was, and kept the fourth box for himself.

Moving through the motions of his day seemed pointless; meetings, conference calls, none of it would matter if he was dying. His shoulder ached even with the pain reliever the doctor gave him. All he could think about was how he was going to break the news to Charlotte and if it made him a complete monster to wait until after the holidays. Maybe he could pretend nothing was wrong until he heard back about the tests. Maybe it was selfish, but he didn't want to give her up yet.

✕

ON MONDAY THE seriousness of her relationship with Caleb settled over her. They'd spent the entire weekend together even though his sister arrived, and yet it seemed completely normal, as if she was always meant to be in his life. They were moving so quickly, and although she had been ecstatic to hear him say they were in a committed monogamous relationship the sober reality made her worry.

She wasn't convinced she could give her heart away again. Although she knew Sam would have wanted her to go on with her life and find love, that was different than her choosing to put herself out there again. If she fully committed to Caleb and let herself fall in love, she was opening herself up to all the heartache that could come with a relationship. Even when both people had the best intentions, someone could get hurt.

Luckily, she was so busy at work that day on her latest project she didn't have much time to dwell on risking her heart again. That evening she was scheduled for a PR team outing at a nail salon. Renee was hosting a final holiday party to thank everyone in PR for all the hard work they'd done that year. They had a private room in a local nail spa reserved, with champagne and appetizers.

Only in New York City would they think to hold a cocktail party while women had their nails done in festive holiday shades. But the party gave her a great excuse to take a break and let Caleb have time with his sister. At seven she was surprised she hadn't heard from him all day and itched to text him just to check in. So much for needing some space.

"Hey boyfriend, how was your day?" she texted.

She waited for a response but had to put her phone away for her nails to get painted.

Thirty minutes later her red nails were dry and she still had no response from Caleb. Maybe he needed a little breathing room too. The rest of the evening faded into holiday games, Christmas bonuses, and Charlotte didn't get home until ten.

Instead of wondering, she called him, and he answered right away but sounded off.

"Hey baby, how was your holiday nail party?" he asked. Of course, he remembered she had an event.

"It was glamorous and over-the-top, just like Renee."

"That sounds fun?" he said, unsure if that was what she considered a good time.

"Yeah, it was fun, but I was wondering how your day was? Did you get a chance to hang out with your sister?"

"She met up with some friends from college, so I just hit the gym after work and was about to head to bed."

"Oh darn I could have come by but maybe a solid night's sleep is in order. You sound tired."

"As much as I love our nights together, I think you're right. I was dragging today. One night apart won't kill us and eight hours of sleep is probably all I need," Caleb said but his tone sounded sad.

"You don't sound convinced, everything okay? It's not too late for me to get a taxi and be there in time to be your personal human blanket."

He chuckled over the phone, and she imagined him already lying in bed with his shirt off and his ab muscles flexing when he laughed.

"That does sound cozy, but it's late. Tomorrow Katie has another night planned with friends. How about we stay in and take turns on being human blankets."

"Deal. Get some sleep tonight, because I predict you'll get very little tomorrow," she said.

"Good night, baby," he said.

"Good night."

She couldn't help but feel like he was holding back. Maybe he just had a bad day at work and was exhausted from all their long nights. Meanwhile, she was regretting ever thinking she wanted some space and not just going to his house after the holiday party. One night away and it was clear she was already more attached to him than she was ready to admit.

Chapter Twenty-Four

CHARLOTTE HAD A small gift to give Caleb, and it was their last night together before she caught the early morning train to Virginia. It had only been a few weeks, but he already seemed entrenched in her heart. If she didn't wake up in his arms, she counted down the minutes until she would see him. They made plans for New Year's Eve, because it was a given that they would spend the evening together. He was penciled into her future, and she liked it.

Her last day in the office until after Christmas flew by as she worked frantically to respond to any outstanding emails and sign off on all the requirements for the current projects. It was six o'clock by the time she made her way through the city to Caleb's apartment.

She'd worn a red wrap dress to work, with tall brown boots and was excited for him to unwrap it and find his other Christmas gift—an obscenely sexy bra and panty set she bought on impulse when she was shopping for him. What did you get the guy you had known for years, but only dated for a few weeks? As she'd walked through one of the largest department stores on her lunch break, she found a snow globe with the Colosseum inside and thought it was a nice way to remember where they met in Rome.

Knocking on the door, she hoped he liked both gifts.

He answered the door with a smile that didn't quite reach his eyes. Leaning forward he enveloped her in a warm hug before he kissed her neck.

"Hi, baby."

The sadness she heard in his voice the night before was still there, and she studied him as he closed the door.

"What's wrong?" she asked unsure if she wanted to hear the answer. His eyes looked anywhere but in hers and she was sure something was very wrong.

Taking her hand, he tried to lead her farther into his apartment, but she stopped, clutching the awkwardly wrapped snow globe to her chest.

"Caleb, what is wrong? You're freaking me out."

He ran his hand through his already mussed hair, and she noticed the more than five o'clock shadow covering his handsome face. His forehead creased as he grimaced.

"I'm sick. I had a spot on my shoulder that turned out to be a melanoma. Cancer. My doctor said they caught it early but needed to do more testing to see if it spread. I know this is horrible timing to tell you right before the holidays but it's not something I can hide. I think the sooner you know the better."

Charlotte stood stunned and didn't realize until the glass shattered that she'd dropped the snow globe.

"I was almost thinking it might be easier for you if I just ghosted you, but I would never want you to think that I didn't want you."

His eyes met hers and the pain she saw was devastating. Her heart felt like it had stopped pumping her blood and her hands tingled.

"At the same time, I would never ask you to go through this with me. You've already been through so much. It's just really terrible timing. If only I'd found out a few weeks ago, I could have spared you all of this." He ignored the broken glass and the puddle from the wrapped snow globe that sat on the ground between them as he stepped closer. "You have to believe me, I never wanted to hurt you, Charlotte."

"You have cancer?" she repeated. Her mind felt like mush and she struggled to catch up to everything he said.

"Yes."

"You have cancer, and you're dumping me? I mean I realize that isn't the worst part of this, but it feels like you're saying you don't want to see me anymore."

Caleb closed the space between them but didn't reach out to touch her. He was close but at the same time as far away from her as he could get. He was shutting her out.

"It's not fair, but it's probably for the best if we just stop things now before this gets too messy. I don't know exactly how bad things will be but after googling melanoma I'm not feeling very positive about it."

"But—" The thought of Caleb having chemo or radiation, losing his hair, losing weight, and getting sick caused her stomach to lurch. She didn't know if she could go through that and then lose him.

She had been devastated that Sam had been taken from her so swiftly; in a matter of moments his life was gone. She never saw him again. But cancer would mean a slow deterioration and Caleb's muscular, healthy, virile body would fade into a ghost of the man before her now.

"I'm not asking you to make a decision, Charlotte. I've already decided I think I should go through this alone. I need to focus on beating cancer, not how you'll cope with it." His eyes bored into hers, but it was like she was looking at someone else.

His words cut like a knife. He didn't want her. Her eyes filled with tears, and she started to reach out to him, but he stepped back. She turned away and walked toward the door. With one look back her vision blurred before the tears overflowed in fat drops down her cheeks.

"You're right about one thing. This isn't fair." It was all she could muster before she let herself out and the heavy door slammed behind her as she ran to the elevator. She had to get as far away from him as possible.

✕

CALEB'S EMOTIONS WERE raw, and yet he was completely detached from his life. After Charlotte left, he cleaned up the smashed gift but didn't have the heart to throw it away. He found a replica of the Colosseum in a pool of glittery liquid. It was the perfect symbol of what he couldn't have. Placing the sad figurine on his nightstand, he locked himself in his room until the next morning. Luckily his sister stayed out late with her friends, and he used work as an excuse the next day to be out of the house. When his parents arrived that evening, he painted on a smile and played the part of a good son. There was no way he was going to crush more people he loved by telling them he might be dying.

Part of him imagined Charlotte would argue with him

and fight him on his plan to break up. He thought in the last three weeks he carved out a place in her heart and she wouldn't be able to leave him to wallow in his depression alone. But he couldn't blame her for running. He'd pushed her, and she had responded defensively.

He wasn't going to fault her for it, no matter how much it hurt. He'd wanted to spare her as much pain as possible and end it before his cancer got worse and the treatments took over his life. Granted he'd lied about not wanting to worry about how she would cope with his illness. But he thought it was the best way to let her off the hook.

He knew Charlotte could be convincing when she wanted to be and if she was up for the fight, she would have stayed. If she had fallen in love with him like he had fallen in love with her, she would have stayed.

It had been three days since he got the diagnosis and he just needed to make it until after Christmas to let himself completely fall apart. He was holding out hope that it hadn't spread and that all this worry was for nothing, but something inside told him he would be disappointed. He needed to be ready for the worst. For now, he was going to enjoy the time with his family and hope for Charlotte's sake she could do the same.

Chapter Twenty-Five

"*B*ABE, HAVE YOU *seen my keys?*" *Sam called out.*

"*Never mind, I found them.*" *Sam's sheepish smile greeted her as she rounded their bedroom door, dripping wet having just jumped out of the shower.*

"*Where are you going? You're supposed to have off this weekend,*" *Charlotte said, trying not to let her voice come out as a strained plea.*

"*The team is still understaffed, and it's been an active Saturday. We have a green light on a raid we've been planning,*" *he said but moved closer pulling her towel where it was knotted. He slowly undid the tie. His eyebrows moved up as he made a low whistle.*

"*On second thought, maybe I can be a few more minutes late.*"

"*That will definitely take longer than a few minutes,*" *she said, feeling her skin heat under his approving eyes before she rewrapped her towel.*

He kissed her like he was desperate to stay, melding his body to hers while his hands framed her face.

Her stomach twisted and turned as a cold chill ran up her spine.

"*I'll be right back,*" *he said, and with a final kiss he walked toward the door.*

"No, you won't. You don't come back," she called out, but Sam just kept walking away from her.

She tried to follow him, but her legs were slow to move.

"Don't go, Sam. Please just stay. If you go, you'll die and I need you," Charlotte yelled but he didn't hear her.

He was gone.

She sank to the floor in her towel and screamed while tears began to stream down her face.

✕

"WHAT DO YOU think the dream means?" Charlotte said, sitting in her PJs in her dark bedroom at her parent's house back in Virginia. It was Christmas Eve and she was back home. After a long day of crying on the train ride the day before then pretending nothing was wrong at dinner with her folks, she'd slept hard.

She hadn't had a dream about Sam in months. She used to call Conner when the weight of losing Sam hit her but she hadn't needed to lately. Rory had always acted as her self-appointed protector, but he also punished himself for Sam's death. Conner was more practical and always brought levity to the situation.

"Honestly?" Conner's groggy voice replied over the phone.

"Yes," Charlotte wiped at her nose that was running from the tears she woke up crying.

"I think your dream is a direct reflection of where you are in your life. You're still holding onto the idea that you never should have had to lose Sam. At the same time, you've developed feelings for Caleb and you're worried about falling in love—and even more terrified to lose someone again."

He already knew about them dating but she left out the part about him ending things. She wasn't ready to admit he rejected her.

Charlotte let out a deep breath. "Ouch."

"I know the truth hurts but so does denying it. We both know you didn't call me at the crack of dawn to sugarcoat this," Conner said.

"No, I didn't," Charlotte agreed.

"I'm going back to sleep. See you later today," Conner said before he hung up the phone.

Charlotte flung back the covers, knowing she wouldn't get any more sleep. After making some hot chocolate she sat in the living room and watched the Christmas lights change from blue to gold and back again. She wondered if she would ever look at a Christmas tree again without thinking about Caleb. Her breath caught at the idea of not seeing him again, not feeling his skin against hers, and she questioned when her feelings for him became so strong. Maybe the threat of losing a person heightened an attachment, or maybe she started falling in love with him the first time he kissed her in Rome. Once they were both finally in New York it sealed her fate.

The sound of scraping ice interrupted her thoughts, and she noticed the sun had risen in the time she sat staring at the tree. Sunlight sparkled through the windows by the door. Looking out she saw Sam's mom attempting to chip the layer of ice that had frozen on her windshield overnight.

After all these years his family still owned the home next door.

Unable to stop herself, she put on her coat and slid on some winter boots her mom kept by the door. She caught a glimpse of herself in the mirror that hung on the wall: pale face, puffy eyes, not her best look. Grabbing a pair of gloves and her dad's scraper, she pulled her hood over her wild hair before heading outside.

Stomping through the icicles that froze on the individual blades of grass, she left a trail of footsteps in the lawn and forced a smile as her former mother-in-law looked up.

"Hello sweetheart, do you believe all this ice?" Diana said, shaking her head. "Sort of a white Christmas, I suppose."

"I didn't expect to see you for some reason. I thought you were living down south for the winter," Charlotte said.

"I should have stayed there, but my sister Jane has a new grandbaby and we decided it would be fun to be the doting grannies for Christmas this year. You remember Sam's older cousin Jenna, baby number three."

"Oh, that's nice." Charlotte started helping her scrape the windshield.

As neighbors for twenty-plus years, her mom would always stay in touch with Sam's mom, but Charlotte felt like they lost their link, or maybe it was too hard for both of them.

"How are you?" Diana stopped chipping at her wipers and looked at Charlotte with kind eyes. "Your mom said you moved to New York. That sounds exciting." Placing her hand on Charlotte's shoulder, she smiled.

She was genuinely happy to see Charlotte, which only made her feel worse for not being better about keeping in touch.

"I'm not sure." She forced a smile under Diana's scrutiny. The remnants of her dream of Sam the last time she saw him sat heavily on her heart. "I sold our condo, took a great job in New York, and even started dating again. But all roads lead back to Sam. He was my person. He was my soulmate," Charlotte said as an emptiness filled her stomach.

Sam's mom tsked and gave Charlotte's arm a squeeze.

"No, he wasn't, honey. I know that may sound harsh, but clearly, fate has another path for you. Although it must be terribly difficult to see it. Sam was a part of your journey, maybe even a major bend in your road—I'd certainly like to think so—but he wasn't the end of your story. It doesn't work that way." Her tone was gentle but forceful at the same time.

"But we were so connected. I loved him so much and he understood me," Charlotte said.

"I'm grateful he found the love of his life in you, Charlotte, but you can't let yourself believe he was the only love of your life. You're too young, and what about children?" Mrs. James said.

"I don't know about that. I don't know if I could ever love someone like that again."

"You mean you're scared because you could get your heart broken again. Trust me, from a woman who has loved and lost, hurt can find you no matter what you do."

Charlotte swiped at an errant tear that fell when she thought about how hard life could be and how some people got more than their fair share of heartbreak. Sam's father had died of a sudden heart attack when Sam was in college, and his mom never remarried. Then she lost her son, and Charlotte was daunted by the idea of how a person could cope with so much pain.

"No one said life would be easy. So go out there and fall in love and enjoy it for as long as it lasts." Mrs. James stomped her foot in emphasis.

Tears rolled down Charlotte's face, and she felt her body shudder before they hugged and both sniffled.

"I don't want to forget him," Charlotte said.

"You won't. How could you when he'll always be with you?"

Sam's mother leaned forward and kissed Charlotte on the cheek before giving her one more hug.

"You can miss him and love someone new. We both know that's what he would want."

Charlotte nodded, knowing it was true. It was like Sam sent his mom to give her permission to forgive herself for falling for someone else.

That evening the annual Maguire Christmas Eve family dinner was complete and now her brothers, several aunts, uncles, and cousins eagerly awaited pie. The house was loud and a hive of activity with her cousin's twin boys running around, several pre-teens on their phones in the living room, and her uncles telling stories of their time on the force. Her grandfather always said: a family of cops was never in need of storytellers; an Irish family of cops was always in need of more whiskey.

Charlotte stood in her parents' kitchen trying to figure

out what went wrong with Caleb while she was supposed to be getting dessert plates. She tried to consider the diagnosis from Caleb's perspective. He always made her feel like she was everything he wanted but maybe finding out he had cancer gave him a moment of clarity. At the same time something he said kept bothering her. *He would never ask her to sit by and watch him get sick.*

"What's up with you? Are we too boring now that you live in New York?" Rory asked as he surveyed the array of desserts their mom labored over. There were several types of pie, cookies, cakes, and the quintessential Jell-O fruit mold which was more of a joke than anything else laid out on the island.

"She's torturing herself over falling in love with the Italian," Conner said, walking up and grabbing a cookie.

Rory's eyebrows lifted in surprise, and he stood straight up from smelling the pie. "Love?"

Charlotte's cheeks heated and her stomach twisted into a knot. Was it so obvious she was in love with Caleb? Why did it take her brother to say it out loud to make it feel so real? Would Rory be disappointed she fell for someone after Sam? She stood mute while Rory studied her.

"I'm happy for you, Charlotte. It was obvious Caleb has been holding a flame for you for a long time. I wasn't sure if you would let yourself fall." Rory came around the other side of the island and gave her a comforting side hug. "But if you're in love, why do you still look so sad?"

Conner stopped chomping his cookie and looked up just as tears filled her eyes and she turned her face into Rory's side. He wrapped her up into a hug before ushering her to move out of the kitchen into the mudroom for privacy. Conner followed with the plate of cookies and then shut the door. Rory gave her another squeeze before he lifted her onto the washing machine and stood back. With a wide-leg stance, he grabbed a cookie, then crossed his arms and stared her down.

"Spill it. What's going on? Did that pretty boy hurt you?" Rory asked.

Conner set the plate of cookies next to her on the dryer and mimicked Rory's stance while holding several additional cookies.

Charlotte rolled her eyes. "No, or yes, but I don't think it was on purpose. In fact, I'm starting to wonder if it was more of self-sacrifice on his part."

"Please start from the beginning," Rory said before taking a huge bite of his cookie.

With a huff Charlotte told them everything: how she gravitated to Caleb at the company holiday party, that they started dating and sleeping together—both her brothers squirmed at that detail. Then she explained her last conversation with Caleb when he told her he had cancer and how cold he had been before he ended it.

"Classic case of Romeo and Juliet," Conner said.

"Wasn't that a story of two idiot teenagers that offed themselves because their families wanted to keep them apart?" Rory said.

Charlotte rolled her eyes and grabbed a cookie. This was like every serious conversation she ever had with her brothers.

"No, it is the story of two people in love and one sacrifices themself so that the other will go on and find someone else to love," Conner corrected.

"That is not how it goes, and Caleb and I are not Romeo and Juliet; neither of us is offing ourselves," Charlotte said, feeling more annoyed by the minute.

"Clearly, but it does sound like Caleb gave you an out, because if he does have cancer—assuming he wouldn't lie about that, he doesn't want you to stay by his side out of honor. He recognizes you have already been through a lot and shouldn't have to watch someone you love suffer."

Her breath caught in her throat and Charlotte's entire body felt numb. "He didn't want to put me through the pain of him having cancer?"

"Very noble and very Shakespearean proof that he loves you," Conner agreed.

"And in return, I made it about myself and rejected him. I thought he was using cancer as an excuse to dump me, so he wouldn't have the stress of dealing with my feelings and my baggage. I didn't even try to argue with him."

Rory and Conner both shook their heads as they each chomped into another cookie.

"I'm a self-absorbed idiot," Charlotte said.

Both her brothers nodded in agreement.

"But it sounds like you're in love with him, and maybe that love blinded you to the fact that Caleb is so in love with you that he would sacrifice his own happiness to make sure he didn't hurt you in any way," Conner said.

Rory punched Conner's arm. "Easy, dude. She's putting it together, don't make her feel any worse."

Conner shrugged. "I never sugarcoat love."

Rory scoffed. "As if you know anything about love and sacrifice."

"As if you do? You're more allergic to a serious relationship than I am. At least I have a pet, proof I can commit," Conner said.

"An outdoor cat does not count as a pet," Rory said.

"I can't believe it took this ridiculous conversation for me to see why Caleb pushed me away. I can't believe I let him think I wouldn't stick by him." She hopped down from the washing machine. "I have to get back to New York."

Rory looked at his watch. "I doubt you'll find a seat on any train tonight and those buses are too dangerous; the roads are all going to be covered in ice."

Charlotte looked out the window and could see the fresh dusting of freezing rain on the grass and the delicate steady flow as hail pelted the ground.

"Poor Caleb. He's probably crying into his yule log wondering how you could be so heartless," Conner said. "If only there was something like a phone you could use to call him and explain how you've been a fool."

This time Charlotte hit Conner. "Smartass." Pushing past her brothers, she went back to the kitchen to find her phone.

That night she stared at Caleb's name in her phone, trying to work up the nerve to call him, but her doubts stopped her. Questions rolled through her mind. Was she capable of coping with cancer? What if it killed him? Telling Caleb she was sorry for not fighting for them, was only one aspect of what stood between them. The real question was, could she handle loving him, standing by him, and possibly losing him? Was she strong enough?

Her questions were an avalanche between them, and she wasn't completely sure he wanted her by his side while fighting cancer. He had pushed her away, but the only way to find out any answers was to talk to him.

Chapter Twenty-Six

C HARLOTTE'S HANDS HADN'T stopped trembling since the weight of her mistake settled over her on Christmas Eve. Unable to get an earlier train back to NYC, she took the first train the day after Christmas. It must have been the worst day to travel, with delays and overbooked trains, but she finally made it to her apartment by evening. After a night of little sleep, she arrived at work as the sun came up. She expected the office to be empty after Christmas weekend since a lot of people were still on leave and celebrating with their families. But there was one person she was counting on being there. Before everything went wrong, he had said as the most junior VP, he was tapped to put in an appearance throughout the holiday.

She would know if he logged into his computer because the company had an internal chat system that showed when a user was online. The only thing she could do was confront Caleb about his real reasons for pushing her away. Was it because he wanted to spare her getting hurt, or was he not interested in something more serious?

Cancer sounded like a big commitment.

She knew his family was staying with him, so her best bet was catching him at work, not exactly professional but she was feeling desperate.

"Charlotte, what are you doing here today?" Her head popped up from her computer to find Renee standing in her office. She wasn't sure how long she had been there, sifting through emails while waiting to see if Caleb's name would pop up.

"After several days with my family, I was eager to get back and start on that new project." She stumbled on her excuse.

"The marketing plans for the three new boutique B&Bs? You know you won't be able to get in touch with anyone in Europe. No one is going to be doing real work until after New Year's," Renee said, walking closer.

In retrospect, she probably should have taken more time with her makeup to cover up the circles under her eyes.

"Are you sure you're okay? The holidays can be difficult," Renee said in an uncharacteristically soft tone.

Before she could respond, a man Charlotte didn't recognize stepped in front of the doorway. "Babe, you ready?"

Charlotte stood and pushed her hair back behind her ear, catching the flirty smile that lit Renee's face.

"I'll be right there." Renee turned back to Charlotte and held up a pair of black stiletto shoes. "I had to stop by to grab these to go with my New Year's dress." She leaned forward and whispered, "He's taking me to Ibiza on his personal jet."

"Wow," Charlotte said, forcing a smile.

"I know. Look, take the rest of the week off or maybe work from home. Take some time for yourself. There is no rule you have to spend the holidays with family. Treat yourself to a much-deserved break." Renee smiled and reached out to squeeze Charlotte's arm in comfort.

"Maybe I'll binge on that new Viking series and sit in my PJs all day," Charlotte said.

"Do it." Renee walked to the doorway. "Happy New Year!"

Charlotte waited until she heard them leave before she slouched back into her seat again. Looking at the clock, she realized it was almost noon and Caleb hadn't logged on. He must have decided to work from home or was still reeling with how to cope with his diagnosis.

Logging off her computer, she considered her options. She didn't even know if he would want to see her, but stalking him at work probably wasn't the best plan after rejecting him. She could still see the disappointment in his eyes when she accused him of not being fair to her. He was protecting her from getting hurt, and in return, she'd turned her back on him.

How could she even begin to apologize for that? Tears clouded her eyes, and she grabbed a few tissues from her desk. Dabbing her eyes, she decided she'd better leave before another colleague saw her.

Twenty minutes later she exited a taxi in front of Caleb's building and stood with her feet rooted to the spot while trying to decide her next move. Should she call him and ask if he was willing to see her? Should she try to use her nonexistent charm and pale face with puffy red eyes to get past the concierge to his apartment and just knock?

She knew his family visited for Christmas and suspected they were still there. She didn't want to cause a scene or embarrass him. Digging her hands, in her pockets she began to pace awkwardly around other pedestrians in the chilly air.

"Charlotte?"

She heard a sweet female voice call her name and looked up to find Katie carrying several bags and walking with a woman who looked like her carbon copy with an added twenty or so years.

"It is you. Merry Christmas." Katie gave her a big hug. "Why are you waiting out here in the cold? Caleb will be ecstatic to see you." Katie winked and hooked her hand through Charlotte's arm before she could even think of a getaway. "Mom, this is Caleb's girlfriend, Charlotte."

Caleb's mom smiled wide and leaned in to give Charlotte a hug, "Happy Holidays, Charlotte. We were so disappointed you were out of town for Christmas, but I'm so happy we got to meet you before we leave tomorrow."

His mom's warmth was almost shocking, but then it struck her Caleb must not have told his family about his diagnosis or that she turned her back on him. They had no clue they were inviting a coward into their midst.

"It's so nice to meet you Mrs. Kincaid."

"Call me Cecilia, please. We're not so formal." His mom gave her arm a squeeze. "Oh my, it is so cold. Let's all go up and have some tea. Katie and I have been baking nonstop. You'll have to try some of our famous Italian cookies," Caleb's mom said.

"I really should have called Caleb before just dropping by," she said as they stepped into the warm lobby. "I got back into town last night and thought I might see him at the office but then remembered you were all still here for the holidays."

"He'll be very happy to see you. He's been so grumpy," Cecilia said as they got into the elevator.

Katie smiled. "I'm sure he would have rather spent Christmas with Charlotte instead of all of us taking over his place."

"I'm sure you're right, but she's here now so we can have a visit. I hope you'll stay for dinner then we can get to know you better," Cecilia said and gave her an encouraging smile.

Before she knew it they were at Caleb's door knocking, and he whipped it open. "I told you to take a key." Caleb's eyes grew big as they settled on her between his mother and his sister who were both smiling as if they brought him a treat.

"Look who we found. Go ahead and thank me now, son." Caleb's mom moved past him and set her bags down. "Frank, come meet Charlotte," his mom called out.

Katie gave her a small push to enter so she moved ahead but stopped to stand next to Caleb where he held the door open. "I'm sorry. I was working up the nerve to call you when your sister spotted me downstairs."

Caleb nodded as he closed the door and then a distinguished man with dark curly hair, big brown eyes, and a warm smile appeared. "Dad, this is Charlotte, Charlotte this is my father, Frank."

She held out her hand to shake his, but he pulled her in for a warm hug, just like Caleb's mother had.

"It's a pleasure to meet you, Charlotte. I've heard a lot about you." He looked from her back to Caleb, but his smile fell a bit when he noticed Caleb wasn't exactly happy to see her.

"Why don't I make some tea and we can cut that pumpkin loaf your mom made."

"Maybe when we get back. I need to get out of the apartment for a bit," Caleb said, grabbing his coat from a hook on the foyer wall.

"Let the young people be, Frank. Come on, I'll show you all the pretty things you got me," Caleb's mom said. "Charlotte, it was lovely to meet you and we'll see you for dinner." His mom smiled warmly at her and then shot Caleb a fierce look. She must have also noticed something was amiss.

Caleb held the door open for her, and he didn't speak until they were in the elevator alone.

"I didn't expect to see you again so soon," he said.

"I'm sorry," she said, emotions swelling in her chest. He looked so sexy and sad. She wanted to tell him she was an idiot and beg for forgiveness but the wall between them seemed as high as Mount Everest.

Caleb's head hung. "For which part?"

The elevator doors dinged open, and they walked into the lobby then outside. The cold air hit her, and she pulled her arms around her waist. "Please look at me," she begged as he stood looking out at the traffic.

"I'm sorry I ran. I'm sorry I let you think for a minute that I could just walk away. The truth is I don't think I could even if you wanted me to." She huffed and swiped at a tear that escaped. He finally looked at her, and she could see the anguish in his eyes, the doubt.

"We can't have this conversation here on the street, and we won't get any privacy at my place," Caleb said.

"I know where we can go." She led Caleb two blocks away to where she shopped with Katie for Christmas decorations when he had hauled the tree back to his place. The pop-up shop doubled as a fancy hot cocoa bar and had a dozen heated tables inside clear tents that looked like snow globes. They took over an empty globe when another couple departed. She wondered how long they could sit there without being interrupted for their order.

Caleb leaned back in his seat with a pained look on his face. "You were saying?"

Rubbing her hands together, she felt the chill even in their heated bubble.

"I screwed up and I'm sorry. I thought you were breaking up with me because you didn't want to have to worry about how I was feeling while dealing with your own feelings and being sick."

"I've been very clear about my feelings for you. That didn't change because I found out I have cancer. But I wasn't sure you were invested enough in us to want to go through this with me. I didn't want you to feel obligated." He held her gaze as he searched for the right words. "I wanted to give you the option to end this before I'm too caught up with cancer treatments. I gave you an easy out to spare us both more pain. I thought if you were really ready to be with me, you wouldn't let me push you away. In less than five minutes, you bolted."

The pain in his eyes was clear, and her heart ached that she had been the cause.

"I thought you were rejecting me, and maybe part of me was too afraid to hear anymore."

"Damn it, Charlotte you're as in love with me as I am with you, but that didn't stop you from walking away the second things got tough." He was careful to keep his voice even as he leaned over the small table.

Her eyes were big from hearing him voice the truth. She did love him and he knew it. His hands gently gripped her palms as nervous energy coursed through him.

"I have been hoping your feelings would catch up to mine from the beginning. I thought if I played along with your casual approach, you would see for yourself. I'm in love with you and you're in love with me. You need to accept it."

Her eyes stared into his, searching for something.

"You love me?" she asked, gripping his hands in hers.

"I think I've loved you from the start, but I knew you were scared to take a chance on love again. Maybe I'm not your soulmate, but I think you've always been mine. Ever since Rome, ever since that first kiss." The tears pooling in her eyes nearly destroyed him. "But love doesn't make cancer go away. Love doesn't mean you're emotionally ready to deal with the worst-case scenario. Yes, it hurts but I'm not mad at you. I'm mad at the circumstances."

She let out the breath she was holding, "Did you find out something more about your diagnosis?"

"Not yet. My doctor said it could take five to ten days to get the results on whether the melanoma has spread and where. Even if it hasn't spread, she said I may need a round or more of some immunotherapy drugs."

"Caleb, I am with you. I will be there every step of the way. I promise I won't freak out again," Charlotte said. "I promise. I realized in the two days we were apart that it's already too late for me, because I'm irrevocably in love with you. Losing you in a breakup would be just like a death. Maybe worse, because I would know you were out there and I would still love you."

He cupped her face in his warm hand and wiped away the tears that spilled down her cheeks. "I'm sorry I pushed you away. I only wanted to protect you from this if it was more than you could handle."

"No more protecting me. I need to know when you're going through something. I want to be your person," Charlotte said before she stood from her seat. Walking around to sit in his lap, she kissed him like it was the last first kiss they would ever have because she wasn't ever giving up on him.

"Um, excuse me, would you two like to order. I'm sorry I didn't see you were a new couple," a young man asked, standing awkwardly outside their globe.

"Two espressos, please," Caleb said.

Charlotte sniffled and buried her face in his neck, "Do we need our energy for something?"

"Yes, you're having dinner with me and my family tonight."

"You didn't tell them, did you?" Charlotte asked.

"No, I didn't want to ruin their holiday. I'll tell them when I have to."

Chapter Twenty-Seven

CALEB UNRAVELED HIS body from the sheets and grabbed his jeans off the floor where he'd discarded them the night before. After dinner with his family, he and Charlotte took a taxi back to her place. They came together like a storm as soon as they made it into her apartment and then both fell asleep exhausted from the stress of the last two days apart. The soft rhythmic sound of her breathing as she slept proved she was wiped out. He leaned over to kiss her cheek, and she still didn't budge.

In the kitchen he found a pad of paper and a pen to leave her a note. He planned to go to work today once he saw his parents off to the airport.

"I didn't want to wake you. I'll be at work by 10 and hopefully see you tonight. Love, Caleb."

He left the note in front of her coffee maker. It was liberating to finally be so open about his feelings for her. No more hiding, they both agreed.

On the ride home, he let the doubt about his future seep in. He expected to hear from the doctor by Friday and that was going to be one of the most monumental conversations of his life. The weight of that settled over him like a dark cloud. He couldn't help but question if Charlotte knew what she was signing up for. How could she when they weren't sure how sick he was going to get? She said breaking up would be worse than death, but he worried she may regret that decision. He may regret letting her back into his life but selfishly he couldn't resist the chance to be with her, even if it couldn't last.

The minute he arrived in the office his phone rang, and the caller ID was his doctor's office.

"This is Caleb," he said as a nervous tremor ran over him.

"Mr. Kincaid, we have your test results back, and the doctor would like to meet with you today."

"I can come right now. I'll be there in twenty-five minutes. Can you at least tell me what the test says?"

"I'm sorry, sir. I don't have access to your results; I just make the appointments. The doctor said to fit you in as soon as you can get here."

Caleb cursed. "Fine, I'm on my way."

On his way back out of the office he texted Charlotte. *My doctor just phoned. I'm headed there now.*

He didn't even bother to tell his secretary where he was going. He didn't know how much he would need to tell work. Everything hinged on what the doctor said. Would he take a leave of absence? Could he work and go through chemo? And did he even want to?

Send me the address. I'll meet you there, Charlotte texted back as he pushed through the throngs of people on the sidewalk and made his way to the train. The traffic was too thick this late in the morning for a taxi to make it the fifteen blocks he needed to get to as fast as possible.

Twenty minutes later he spotted Charlotte running down the sidewalk in her heels to meet him at the medical center.

"You didn't have to run here," he said, unable to stop from smiling at her flushed cheeks.

"I didn't want you to go in alone." She huffed to catch her breath.

He enveloped her in a hug and kissed her. "Thank you."

She clutched his hand in a vise grip as they made their way through the lobby. They were both silent on the elevator ride up. He wasn't sure which of them was more nervous as he checked in at the desk and she fidgeted behind him. She smoothed her jacket and suit pants several times as her breath finally steadied and a forced smile lit her face.

Sitting next to her in the stiff waiting room chairs, his stomach was in knots but he was grateful she was with him.

"No matter what happens, I love you and we will beat this." Her voice cracked and her eyes glossed over, but she held back her tears and kissed him just as his doctor opened the door to the patient area.

"Mr. Kincaid, come on back, please," his doctor said, holding a file.

The tone of her voice was not good. His legs were heavy as he stood, and he couldn't help but think this was going to be a horrible day.

After ushering them into her office, the doctor put some x-rays up on the wall light and shut the door. Charlotte introduced herself without moving from his side, and they both sat down. The doctor leaned against her desk close enough for him to see the strain in her face, and he was struck by how young she was. It must be the nature of her job that made her seem older.

"Mr. Kincaid, we didn't get it all. Today we need to schedule the dissection of your lymph nodes in the area surrounding the original cancer site. I know this is daunting, but we caught this early and there are several types of therapies to attack this once we know the extent of it," the doctor said.

He tried to focus on what she was saying but his breath was caught in his throat, his hands shook, and a chill ran over his body. He could see the doctor's mouth moving but he didn't hear a thing. Everything was mute as the word cancer played over in his mind.

Charlotte waved her hand in front of the doctor. "Excuse me, Doctor, I'm sorry can we just have a second."

She turned to face him. Clutching his hand, she said his name but it sounded all jumbled in his brain. Her cool, dainty hand touched his skin, and she turned his chin to face her.

"Caleb, we're going to beat this." She shook her head up and down as if it were a done deal, as if they had beat a dozen other things as a team. Taking a few deep breaths, she stared into his eyes, imploring him to breathe with her.

He exhaled a whoosh of disappointment.

With a final squeeze, she let go of his hand and dug into her bag to retrieve a notebook and pen.

"Okay, Doctor, let's start from the beginning. Can you explain how you biopsy a lymph node?" Charlotte flipped open her notebook and put the date at the top of the paper, then sat poised to listen.

In the next thirty minutes, she took pages of notes, asked questions, and discussed getting other opinions. She challenged the doctor in a respectful way by asking if it were her loved one getting this diagnosis who she would go to, who was the best.

The doctor acknowledged there were trials through several universities and numerous physicians with world-renowned studies of this very cancer. She had studied under one of them. She also outlined the success rate of the treatment plan she recommended.

"Mr. Kincaid, I am not a fan of sugarcoating a cancer diagnosis. Even with the best statistics and the mildest diagnosis, patients have been lost. However, I will say as your doctor, I feel optimistic that with this treatment plan and the stage of your cancer, you can beat this." She turned to Charlotte. "I can't overstate the importance of a positive mindset and an emotional support system."

Charlotte nodded and closed her notebook, her hand immediately settling on his thigh and she gave him a squeeze.

"So once you've decided, I can perform the biopsy of your lymph nodes on Friday. Our dedicated nursing staff will review the process and time needed for the procedure."

Caleb nodded. "Thank you, Doctor."

"Remember, this is your health, Mr. Kincaid, and you need to decide what is best for you. If you want more time to think things through and get second opinions, I, of course, understand and we can delay the procedure."

"I plan to pore over this information and talk with Charlotte about everything, but I would like to move forward with your plan," Caleb said firmly.

He didn't want to lose another day if there was more cancer in his system. "Not exactly the way we planned to spend New Year's Eve but I don't want to delay it," he said to Charlotte.

"I am 100% on board with that; the sooner we know what we're facing the sooner you kick cancer's butt." Her confidence helped more than she could know.

The doctor nodded and stood. "Then we'll see you Friday."

✕

CHARLOTTE'S HAND WAS cramped from writing notes, her stomach was growling, and her head throbbed from all the tears she forced back as the doctor described his cancer and treatment. She had seen Caleb's text just as she exited her apartment after sleeping in and didn't even call work to tell them she would be late. She considered taking a mental health day but assumed the last thing Caleb would want to do is sit around his apartment and freak out about his diagnosis.

They were both quiet as they exited the medical center, but as soon as they were outside, he pulled her into his arms and the tears she fought so hard began to fall.

"Thank you for doing that with me and being so on top of all the questions I was too distracted to think of." Caleb rubbed her back and she just let the tears come. The sounds and smells of the city wafted around them, but she held on to him for dear life.

Even though it was thirty degrees out, they stood in a ray

of sunshine on the crowded sidewalk and gave warmth to each other. Caleb was her person now. He was sick and she was terrified.

"You never have to thank me for being there for you. Of course I wanted to be with you." She pulled back to look him in the eyes and saw the fear. It broke her heart in a way she never considered.

"Caleb, you're going to beat this. Should we take the day off and review the information your doctor provided? You need time to process this."

He took a deep breath. "I do, but I barely put in any hours this week with the holiday and my parents' visit. I need to get a handle on things in the office and talk to my bosses about taking more time off on Friday." Taking her hand, he guided her toward the train.

"Okay, but I'm coming over tonight," she said.

"Deal."

As they approached their office building, Caleb still held her hand and she didn't let go until she had to exit the elevator to her floor which was several levels below the executive offices.

"I'll see you this evening," she said, squeezing his hand and kissing his cheek. She didn't care if anyone in the office knew anymore. They didn't have time to waste on hiding their relationship.

No one seemed to notice she'd taken off the morning since it was that weird time between Christmas and New Year's. Renee was out of the country until next week and Nina drove to see family in upstate New York. She enjoyed having the office mostly to herself but struggled to focus on work and not go down the internet rabbit hole of researching melanoma and all its stages.

At five o'clock she could see Caleb was still signed onto the computer and she set aside her work. She looked up several of the studies the doctor cited and the holistic therapist that was recommended to keep his mind and body healthy during the treatment. She discovered chemo was basically poison that would kill the cancer cells but immuno-therapy was less invasive. He would be tired, lose weight due to a lack of appetite, experience mood swings and fatigue.

Charlotte knew it was going to be a horrible experience, but she couldn't possibly lose him without a fight. She never got a chance to fight for Sam or even say good-bye. She never got to stress to him how much she loved him before he died, and she wasn't going to lose a single minute with Caleb. Even if it meant loving him and still losing him.

"Knock knock." Caleb stood at her door, and she realized the sun was setting outside, casting pink light into her office.

"Hi, I didn't realize how late it was." She stood and gathered several articles she printed for him.

"What's all that?" he asked, walking farther into her office.

He didn't care if anyone knew about them dating either, if he was visiting her. She smiled at the idea of not having to hold back in their relationship in any way anymore.

"Just a little light reading on chakras and homeopathic herbal remedies. Have you ever done acupuncture? I've always wanted to try it, and I read a fascinating article on the health benefits. I'm making us an appointment." Looking up, he had a big smile on his face before he leaned in to kiss her neck, his signature move.

"I love it when you do that," she breathed, leaning into the kiss.

"You do? What else do you love?" He set his winter coat down on the back of her chair as she stood. Then he slid his hands over her hips to pull her into his body.

"Well, I love your mouth anywhere on my skin, I love how you make my stomach clench right before your hand slides into my panties, and…" she whispered into his ear as she ran her hand up into his hair.

His mouth stopped its path up her throat to her ear. "…and," he prompted.

"And I love you."

He groaned. "Not half as much as I love you."

His mouth was on hers before she could beg, and she hiked up her skirt as he leaned into her against her desk. His thigh pushed her legs apart and he pushed her blazer off her shoulders. He untucked her blouse before running his hand down her abdomen to slip his hand between her legs. She panted and nearly fell forward when he stepped back.

Before she could complain, he stepped away to shut her office door. Hearing the click, she smiled knowing what was next. In two strides he was back in front of her but sunk to his knees. Pushing her skirt up over her hips his hot breath was on her, teasing her. Balancing her weight on her hands behind her on the desk, her head fell back. Slowly he pulled her sheer tights over her hips, down her thighs to rest on her ankles. He slipped each of her shoes off to remove them in an agonizingly slow process. Finally, he pulled her panties down the same path, and she looked down to see his lips spread in a wicked smile before his mouth enveloped her.

Her body exploded with sensations and a warm clenching brewed low inside, waiting for his next touch to build more pressure.

"You're the sexiest man I have ever met," she whispered, running her hand through his thick curls.

"Shhh, I'm busy." The vibration of his mouth on her sensitive skin sent her head back.

Soon he was delving into her with such exquisite force, she was lost in the storm of his dedication to making her body his. Every part of her belonged to him as if his name were written on her soul. Her orgasm was fast, and the shockwaves of pleasure pulsed as he stood in front of her, his breathing heavy. She unbuckled his belt and pushed his pants down just in time for him to push inside her.

"I love everything about you." With every moan he pulled from her he rewarded her with praise. "I love your taste, I love your moans, and I love your body."

Her legs wrapped around his waist as he leaned forward and drove them both over the edge with their desire and emotions exploding in the quiet of the room.

Once they each caught their breath, she couldn't help but laugh as she looked up at the dimmed track lighting of her office. "This is a first," she said.

"Good, but it won't be the last. We still have my office to explore, and I'm thinking of setting up a home office now that I can see the multiple uses." Caleb said.

She enjoyed his sense of humor and for a few moments forgot about cancer. She forgot all the stress of the day. They were just two people loving each other. Creating more moments like this with him was going to be high on her list of to-dos. He needed to concentrate on his treatment, and she wouldn't let either of them wallow in the struggle that would come.

With adoring patience, he helped her get dressed. Once they had their clothes on, she grabbed the stack of articles she wanted to give him and they made their way back to his place.

They ordered their favorite comfort food from a local Thai restaurant and snuggled on the couch. She got the sense that he needed one normal night after the breakup, the holiday, the makeup, and the cancer diagnosis. That night as they got into bed, she could feel the worry they both had about the future but instead of letting it fester, she made love to him until he was too tired to worry. At first, she struggled to fall asleep, but eventually the sounds of his deep breathing coaxed her.

Chapter Twenty-Eight

ON FRIDAY MORNING Caleb got out of bed as usual when the sun came up and ran through his normal routine. Even though he was supposed to fast before his procedure later that morning, he brewed half a pot of coffee. Charlotte would want at least two cups before they made their way to the medical center. He washed and cut fruit for her while oatmeal cooked on the stove.

"Are you a glutton for punishment or did you forget you have to fast?" She asked walking into the living room.

Looking up, he smiled at her standing in his T-shirt from the day before and her bedhead of wild hair. She looked like a goddess, a siren ready to tempt him to crash his ship on her shores and he was more than willing to.

"Good morning. I wanted to stay busy, and you need to stay energized. We both know you get a little grouchy when you skip breakfast."

"I don't know what you mean. I'm always completely pleasant," she said as she poured a cup of coffee and bumped him with her hip.

After filling a bowl with hot oats and fresh berries on top, he slid it in front of her.

"Eat," he said, trying to sound stern but it ended with a

smile as her mouth pursed. He could see the desire in her eyes as she set down her cup. Her arms wrapped around his waist, and he couldn't resist as her body melded to his.

"I love when you're bossy in the kitchen," she breathed before she leaned up to kiss him with full force.

Mint and coffee met his lips as he deepened the kiss. He didn't know if she was trying to distract him, but it was clear she was hungry and it wasn't for oatmeal. Caving to Charlotte's desire while he still had the energy wasn't a hard decision and they soon unraveled. With every caress, he hoped she could feel his adoration of her and appreciation that she would be standing by him.

An hour later they exited their taxi and arrived in the cancer treatment wing where he would receive a briefing on the process. Charlotte took more notes, and when he needed to select a next of kin while in treatment, she volunteered before he had to ask.

"It makes the most sense to put me down since I plan to be with you for each of the in-office treatments. Your family all live too far away, and I can always call them if there's some freak emergency." She brushed off the possibility that his body could turn on him completely and shut down once the medicine took over.

Later that afternoon when they returned to his apartment, he didn't feel drained from the procedure as much as the stress and expectation of knowing he was now officially a cancer patient.

"I think I'll take a nap and just lay low the rest of the day. Are you planning to go into the office?" He sat on the bed and lay back, noticing the hunger he had that morning was gone.

"Nope, I'm staying until you kick me out, so it could be a long weekend for you. You might even regret letting me finagle my way into your life." Charlotte smiled and pulled the covers up over him on the bed before sitting next to him.

Taking her hand, he kissed the inside of her palm. "I could never regret you. Thank you for being here."

"I'll be set up in the living room with my laptop and do a little work while you rest."

He nodded and smiled as his eyes began to feel heavy. He could hear her pad out of his room and then come back. Fighting to open his eyes, he watched as she set a full glass of water, a pack of crackers, and a bowl on his nightstand. Then she kissed his cheek before she left the room.

✕

CHARLOTTE COULDN'T DECIDE if she should let Caleb sleep or wake him for dinner. She suspected he was going to get sick when he woke up, but she had simple broth simmering on the stove for him. Although it was tough to focus after an intense morning, she managed to get a little work done while he slept. Then she set up his living room with a few New Year's Eve decorations, large silver and black balloons filled with confetti, a New Year's sign, and a few noisemakers. Instead of a fancy meal, she planned an array of mild comfort foods, ice cream, and a mocktail toast.

Sitting in the waiting room while Caleb's doctor performed the removal of his lymph nodes had been excruciating and only solidified how right it felt to be with him. She had a lot of time to mull over their atypical romance and felt sure on some level they had always been meant to be. Sam had played a huge part in her life, and she would always miss him but she couldn't stop the magnetic pull she felt when she was with Caleb. She had felt certain she belonged with Sam when she married him, but now she couldn't imagine not loving Caleb or spending her life without him.

"Is there anything you can't do?" Caleb said from the bedroom doorway.

Staring out the window at the city that twinkled in the early evening dark blue sky she hadn't heard him get up. Moving into action, she walked into the kitchen barefoot and her fancy cocktail dress swished.

"That is some dress," he said as his hand moved to his stomach.

Twisting her hips, the full pleated tulle skirt covered in sequins swished and sent sparkles across the floor. "Your sister helped me pick it out. I went with an over-the-top vibe," she said, lifting the top off of the pot and releasing the delicious smell.

"Did you decorate the apartment, get dolled up, and make me soup? Did I already die and go to heaven?" he asked as he met her in the kitchen.

"Not funny, but yes to soup and decorating. Just because we're staying in for our first New Year's Eve together doesn't mean we shouldn't celebrate." She ladled soup into a bowl, then placed it in front of him at the counter. "Now eat."

"Who's the bossy one? He passed the seat with the steaming bowl of soup at the island and pulled Charlotte into his warm, strong arms before placing a kiss on her neck.

"I love you," Caleb whispered as his mouth moved over her neck and he lifted her off the ground in a fierce embrace.

"I love you too."

Pulling back, she ushered him to sit down and eat.

After he devoured his soup, Charlotte walked him into the living room to sit on the couch where she had several blankets waiting.

"We're going to have a romantic, snuggly evening and a special countdown for two." She lit candles, turned on the gas fireplace, and poured sparkling grape juice in their champagne flutes.

"I'll have to try to top this next year," Caleb said, watching as she finally sat next to him.

Handing him a full flute, she laughed. "Good idea, we could take turns outdoing each other every year," she said, sitting next to him.

Sitting side by side with their thighs pressed together, and their faces only a few inches apart she could see the hope in his eyes.

"Instead of making a toast, how about we make a promise," he said. "I promise to never hide my feelings from you again and to love you," Caleb said, holding up his purple-tinted sparkling glass.

Her eyes brimmed with fresh tears because of all the promises she wanted, she knew he couldn't promise to live forever.

"I promise to tell you when I freak out and love you back."

They clinked their glasses and both sipped their drinks.

"Baby, you can freak out, as long as you freak out with

me," he said.

Pressing her lips to his, she looped her free arm around his shoulder to pull him closer. He didn't need any further encouragement and deepened the kiss into a mind-numbing, passionate embrace. Charlotte was terrified to lose someone again but the idea of not being with Caleb was worse.

Caleb's hand slid over her chin to cup her face and he kissed her gently with adoration.

"Does this mean you're ready to tell your family about us?" he asked with a hint of mischief in his voice.

"Are you ready to deal with my brothers?"

"I can handle the Maguire brothers. They've got nothing on you and your stonewall tactics. I practically had to beg you to date me."

"And now look what you've done. You're stuck with me!"

It was amazing to feel so loved again and liberating to let herself feel all the passion and hope. She'd been tied to Caleb since Christmas but didn't understand how to acknowledge it or how to be the person he needed. Cancer and his attempt to set her free forced her to see how much they meant to each other.

Her heart was with Caleb, and she was going to enjoy every day they were blessed to have together. She couldn't hold back her feelings for him anymore and she didn't want to.

Charlotte finally understood she had to forget Sam a little to make room in her heart for Caleb, but she knew Sam would forgive her.

Fate gave her a second chance at love, and life could be too short to squander it.

Epilogue

CHARLOTTE TOOK A deep breath before she walked around the front of the car. The stones in the driveway crunched under her feet, and the cool breeze pushed the tall green grass to wave. She fought the butterflies in her stomach, and the desire to laugh at her nervous energy.

Caleb opened the passenger door and stretched his tall body from the compact car.

"I'm sorry they didn't have a roomier car. It's so odd they were sold out for Columbus Weekend. Are your legs sore?"

"I'm fine. You gotta stop worrying." Caleb pulled her into a hug. "Remember I have a clean bill of health. It's time for me to worry about you now."

Her knee-jerk reaction since January was to worry about Caleb's comfort when he started treatment after they found cancer in several lymph nodes. Fast forward ten months, two more surgeries, many tests, and he was in remission. But his body was still recovering from cancer and the treatments. Putting on muscle again required a strict diet and gym routine, but the fatigue had lasted long after his treatments. It had been six months since his last dose and he looked healthy, but she could tell the entire experience took its toll.

"Don't be worried. Everyone already loves you," she said,

noticing he seemed edgy as they got closer to her folks' lake cabin. It was the annual Maguire family weekend and all three of her brothers planned to attend.

"I'm not worried. Rory said they would go easy on me," he said sarcastically.

She paused in grabbing her bag from the backseat to study him. "When did you speak to my brother?"

"We talk from time to time. Mostly about golf or food, but he manages to slide in a few protective big brotherisms now and then," Caleb said, grabbing their two bags from the trunk and avoiding her eyes.

"I didn't realize you two exchanged numbers."

"I have to maintain some mystery," he said, before kissing her long enough to distract her.

Rory, Conner, and her parents had visited them multiple times in the months after Caleb's diagnosis. They doted on them both and accepted Caleb into the family without hesitation.

"Ready?" he asked from the top step of the family cabin.

"Mom is going to be ecstatic," Charlotte said, grabbing the front door knob.

"You didn't tell her anything did you?"

She moved closer, enjoying the heat of his body before kissing his neck and then his full lips. His hands were busy holding their luggage, and he groaned when she bit his lower lip.

"No, I haven't told a soul." Charlotte pushed open the door and the sound of arguing met their ears.

✕

CALEB TOOK A deep breath as he followed Charlotte into her family cabin. He set their bags by the door and could already hear evidence that her brothers beat them there.

"Dude, I can beat you in a race with a blindfold and one hand tied behind my back." Conner came into sight as he towered over Rory who was nonchalantly sitting at the kitchen counter watching their dad season something.

They were interrupting the latest battle between the brothers, but Caleb hoped it wasn't too late to get in on whatever competition they were arguing about.

"I bet I can beat you both." All three Maguire brothers turned and started laughing.

"Easy does it, Caleb; you're not family yet," Rory said, spinning his stool to face them with a smile.

"We won't be going any easier on you when you are," Conner said.

"Is that what you call that black diamond skiing route Finn has planned for the family ski trip this winter?" Caleb said, walking over to shake Finn's hand. Charlotte's youngest and by far bravest brother had just finished his time in the Navy.

"Clearly I misjudged the ski skills you developed living in Europe. You can stick to the bunny slopes if you want," Finn said.

"Caleb can be on my team for today's festivities, so winners versus you and Finn," Conner said, putting his arm around Caleb's shoulders and staking his claim.

"You should have pretended to be the more cerebral type around these three alphas, Caleb. Now they'll pull you into all of their competitions." Charlotte's mom gave him a hug and a big kiss on the cheek. Her dad shook his head.

"Nah, I always wanted brothers," Caleb said.

"Maybe Caleb wants to relax a bit or help me on the grill while you fools try to one-up each other," Charlotte's dad said.

"No," all three of the Maguire brothers said in unison.

"What about you, Charlotte? Are you going to join our annual Maguire relay race?" Rory asked.

Charlotte looked at Caleb with a big smile, and a blush began to creep up her neck as she took his hand.

"Not this year. I think I need to be a little more careful." She rubbed her hand over her growing belly under the flowy yellow sundress she wore, then looked to her mom.

With a gasp, her mom enveloped her in an embrace while her brothers looked confused.

"A baby?" her mom gushed, and Charlotte's eyes filled with tears.

Rory stood to shake Caleb's hand as the other Maguire men crowded around them.

"This isn't the news I was expecting, but I'm not ashamed to tell you it might be even better," Charlotte's dad came around the island and embraced Caleb before hugging Charlotte.

Once the initial buzz quieted, Caleb cleared his throat and grabbed Charlotte's hand. "Now that you mention it, Mr. Maguire, there was something else I was hoping to announce this weekend." Caleb got down on one knee with her family surrounding them and presented a red velvet box to Charlotte as her eyes grew huge with surprise. "Charlotte, you were willing to love me for my whole life, no matter how short that could have been. I love you. Please say you'll be my wife. Marry me?"

The room was completely silent as Charlotte's voice caught in her throat over the tears, and she nodded her head up and down before she squeaked out a, "Yes!"

Caleb stood and slipped the sparkling ring on her finger.

The room exploded with cheers as she jumped into his arms and kissed him.

"I don't know how it's possible but I think I love you a little more every day," Charlotte said.

Rory popped the champagne Caleb asked him to bring and Charlotte held up her left hand. A Kincaid family heirloom his mom gave him sparkled on her finger, a dazzling gold band with an emerald-cut diamond.

"A wedding and a baby," Charlotte's mom squealed. "Caleb will be my favorite for years!"

"I guess we better go easy on him now," Conner said. "He really took one for the team giving Mom and Dad their first grandbaby."

"Not just one," Charlotte said.

"Twins," Caleb said, placing his hand on her belly and kissing her neck as she smiled. The room exploded with cheers again as he captured his wife-to-be and babies in a warm hug.

The End

Don't miss the next book in the Legacy of the Maguires series, *Battle of Hearts*!

Join Tule Publishing's newsletter for more great reads and weekly deals!

Acknowledgments

Thank you to my readers for taking a chance on a
new author!
Thank you to my amazing publisher, fantastic editor, and
the wonderful Tule Publishing Team, you've made my
author dreams come true. A huge high-five and thank you to
my four critique partners, who helped me make my stories
better with kindness and constructive critiques. Thank you
to my sister and all the women in my life who always
supported me by reading early unedited drafts, or cheering
me on. Finally thank you to my family, especially my
indulgent husband for letting me spend hours and hours
with my words, lost in my stories. XOXO

If you enjoyed *Last First Kiss*,
you'll love the next book in the…

Legacy of the Maguires series

Book 1: *Last First Kiss*

Book 2: *Battle of Hearts*
Coming in April 2023

Available now at your favorite online retailer!

About the Author

Author of your next binge-worthy romance series, Stella has been plotting sexy, tear-jerker stories since she was old enough to hold a pencil. Born a Georgia peach, Stella loves all things country but calls the beach home even though she's currently living outside D.C. with her family. Most days she can be found drinking too much coffee, collecting lipstick she forgets to wear, and baking.

Thank you for reading

Last First Kiss

If you enjoyed this book, you can find more from all our great authors at TulePublishing.com, or from your favorite online retailer.

TULE
PUBLISHING